# A LOVE SONG FOR REBELS

---

RIVALS #2

PIPER LAWSON

Content editing by Becca Mysoor
Line and copy editing by Cassie Roberston and Joy Editing
Cover design by Lori Jackson
Cover photography by Regina Wamba

# Tyler

*SEPTEMBER*

A seventeen-year-old girl once told me I don't feel enough.

She was wrong.

Am I walking around with a flashing neon sign pointing at my heart saying, "Fuck me over. Here's how"? No.

But heading into the grand auditorium at Vanier with a crowd of students my first day of second year, I feel plenty.

"The demo was great, and you know it," I state

into my phone, talking loudly to be heard above the noise of the crowd.

"Ty, it's not the right time," Zeke answers flatly.

I rub a hand over my neck. It still feels strange not to have hair curling over a collar, but the black Henley suits me better than Oakwood's tailored shirts.

"Is it ever gonna be the right time?"

"Some people wait a lifetime for a chance. You had a golden opportunity, and you fucked up."

My stomach clenches, but the record exec continues. "I could use you Thursday. The studio'll reach out. You're on my radar, kid. Don't make the same mistake twice."

He clicks off, and I barely resist chucking my phone into the throng of students.

"Smile, Ty. This is for posterity." My roommate's drawl shakes me back to the room.

Beck wedges himself next to me, his phone screen trained on us as we make our way toward some seats midway back.

"I'm Beck, and thank you for following my adventures at Vanier. We're at twenty thousand subscribers, and I appreciate you. Today's the first day of second year. For you math nerds, yes, that means final year for those of us in a two-year program, and it's gonna be epic."

He flips the camera outward to survey the scene. The auditorium's a vast, sweeping space with a thousand upholstered seats. When you see it empty, it's like a field waiting for battle.

The stage could be mistaken for part of that battlefield, but it isn't.

It's the prize.

Beck's narrative continues. "First day of a new year means assembly, which is a chance to remind us how lucky we are to live in dorms or rodent-overrun apartments with barely enough time to practice for the survival jobs we're gonna need when we graduate."

His easy deadpan has me lifting a brow. Usually Beck's a hundred percent optimism even when I'm not.

"You're cheery after the long weekend," I note.

"Came out to my parents. For future reference, Labor Day party in Southampton is a bold choice for announcing you're bi." He looks between the camera and me. "On the plus side, everything I own from home will be in our apartment by tomorrow. Including a kickass Bluetooth speaker.

The bass will blow your mind… and almost make up for the fact that our fridge broke this morning."

I want to ask him about the coming out part, but the recording light's still on.

We turn down a row of seats partway back, moving past second years like us and the wide-eyed freshmen.

I refuse to believe we were that naïve a year ago.

"Even if I gave a shit what my parents think, there's no going back. Guys give better head," my roommate goes on, tripping over classmates as we pass. "Girls are enthusiastic, but a dude knows how to treat a dick."

In the middle of the row, I grab his phone, hit the Stop button, and hand it back amidst his protests. "Beck. Seriously. Tell me you're okay."

His grin is lightning quick, but it takes a moment for him to respond. "I will be," he says at last, clapping me on the shoulder.

I drop into a seat. He takes the one next to me.

"What's new with Cap'n Z?" He nods in the general direction of the cell phone stuck in my pocket.

"Still won't offer me a new deal."

I could be cutting albums right now instead of busting my ass on etudes for class.

Beck frowns. "You should've told him what happened with your dad after you moved to New York."

My entire body stiffens, and I flex my hand on the arm of my seat. It's been months, but mentioning those events still affects me. Maybe it always will.

"Zeke is business. Last year was personal."

When I left Dallas and moved to New York last summer, I'd thought there was nothing left in me to break.

I was wrong. Less than a month later, life brought me to my knees.

The one silver lining is that I poured all my feelings into music. I'm better than I've ever been, and I want to get the hell out of this place. I've had enough of school, enough of people telling me what to do and how to be.

"So, I signed up to be a peer mentor this year," Beck announces. "Got any tips on educating the next generation?"

I shift back in my seat, scanning the rows of students. "Don't fuck whoever's assigned to you."

"Appreciate the input. I'm gonna play that one

by ear. You got some nerves to burn off yourself, roomie," he continues. "You keep way too low a profile. And you're gonna have to start paying me to keep out all the dreamy-eyed people showing up at our door. 'Tyler around? I need to talk to him about class, the state of the Middle East, the state of my bikini wax...'"

His exaggeration makes me laugh.

Yes, I've had my share of offers, but it's been a while since I took a girl up on one.

It's ironic because with all the pent-up energy that's been building lately, I could fuck someone.

God, could I fuck someone.

For an hour, a day, a month, until I forget the resentment and frustration and emptiness.

Most of the people around here would get that I don't want a relationship.

It's like the Olympic Village, an entire community of hot, young, ambitious men and women who need to burn off steam. But at the end of the day, they're here for one reason—to build a career, a future that's brighter than what we came from.

The lights dim, and we train our gazes on the stage.

Vanier is nothing if not theatrical. The college

has a rolling slate of A-list guest faculty including musicians, actors, and dancers.

Today, several of them perform, and Beck's phone peeks up between the heads. I wonder what he's going to edit this into later for mass consumption.

Finally, the dean—herself a former principle ballerina with a national company—clears the stage for her remarks. "Vanier has the nation's most prestigious performing arts programs. We are steeped in tradition, a history of commitment and discipline.

"Some would say technology holds the key to the future, but we believe the arts are more important than ever in these troubled times. Where there is dark, there is also light, and we are seeking to reinterpret this world of struggle, of inequality, of burgeoning possibility and hope, through the lens of the arts."

I'm not here to reinterpret the world.

*I'm going to find a way to get my contract back if it kills me. Starting today, I won't rest until I do.*

The decision fills me with resolve.

My gaze locks on two girls a few rows up, and I tune out the dean's words.

They're both pretty from the back—whatever

the hell that means—but it's the dark-haired girl who has me straightening.

Her hair falls in waves, a shiny river that ends somewhere below her seatback. The glimpse of profile when she turns to listen to something the blonde whispers shows full lips, a pointy nose.

I lean forward as if doing so will let me see more of her.

She's wearing some kind of tight, dark sweater that makes me want to check the rest of her out.

Every part of my body tingles, the frustration transmuting smoothly into attraction.

I haven't felt this way since I saw a ghost nearly four months ago.

*Hallucinations—another reason I need to get the hell out of here.*

"Apparently, my roommate, Tyler, has taken up crack over the summer."

I blink at Beck's phone in my face, and I realize the assembly's done and everyone's getting up to head for class or their dorms or apartments.

As we file out of our row, I scan the bodies ahead of us for the girl I was watching.

I can't find her. The disappointment is stupid because I've never even met her, but there was something magnetic about her.

Classmates stop us to say hi or ask about our summers. Neither Beck nor I have class for half an hour, so we catch up.

I think I've lost track of my roomie when Beck grabs my arm, his face lighting up. "Hey, Ty! I got someone you gotta meet."

He tugs on me. "I told you I was a mentor," he says, pulling to a stop near the doors. "Here's my mentee."

I stop next to him, and my entire body stiffens.

The girl I was checking out is wearing black boots and painted-on jeans that make my abs clench. The sweatshirt's short enough to show a tantalizing sliver of her waist.

Her hair is longer than I thought, and I'm suddenly deciding how many times I could wrap it around my hand.

But when I see her face, every muscle in me tightens.

Full lips, small nose, bright-amber eyes fringed with dark lashes. She's brand new and so familiar I ache.

If there's one small mercy?

It's that Annie Jamieson, the girl I was mentally jerking off to all assembly, looks as stunned as I feel.

2
———

# *Annie*

"**H**ow many of the guys here eat pussy?" Elle, the blonde girl in the room next to mine who introduced herself when I moved in last night, asks from the seat next to me when the assembly concludes.

"Half," I decide.

"Then of the three hotties I spotted while the dean was waxing poetic about tradition, one-point-five might go down on me."

I laugh as the house lights go up.

"I'll even share with you," she says generously as we rise from our seats.

"Do I get the point-five or the whole one every other weekend?"

"Depends how interesting you wind up being."

The theater is huge and full, and I try not to be intimidated as I follow her out of our row. "So, no boyfriend you left behind in Nebraska," I say, remembering our conversation from last night.

"Nope. I do comedy, so everything in my life gets put on display. Guys say they're cool with it, but the first time you tell a room of people about how you found him jerking off to Meryl Streep, it gets strained fast. You want to be a musician, right?" she goes on without pausing for breath.

"Yeah."

"Tell me you're not waiting to get 'discovered.'" She uses air quotes. "Because unless you have contacts or crazy-rich parents, that shit does not work."

My stomach flips over, the excitement I've been feeling tinged with dread.

"My parents don't know I'm at Vanier," I admit. Without meaning to, I feel for the phone wedged into the front pocket of my skinny jeans tucked into black suede ankle boots.

Elle holds a hand in front of her mouth, mock aghast. "Well, now you're getting interesting."

I shake my head as she links arms with me, and we flow toward the door.

When I got admitted to Vanier, I decided not to tell anyone here that I'm Jax Jamieson's daughter.

I'm in a new city with a fresh start I desperately need. I've built my skills and my confidence. This is my chance to prove it to myself and the world.

But this morning's assembly in the huge auditorium is a reminder that there are a thousand other students who want exactly the same thing, and we're competing for mentorship and attention and funding.

On top of which... I lied to my dad and Haley about where I was going to school. The fact that he'd transferred the money for tuition directly to me, like I'd asked, made it easier.

It also made me feel guiltier.

A familiar face near the doors is a lifeline.

"Hey, Beck!" I call, and the dark-haired guy I met at orientation yesterday turns toward my voice.

He has a few inches on me, a broad and infectious grin, and sparkling eyes. He knows he's good looking, and he wants the world to enjoy it as much as he does.

"Hey, Annie. You survived assembly. That's the first hurdle. The next is to keep your mouth shut while these people brag about how epic they are."

I laugh. "Be deferent. Got it."

"Hold on a sec. Don't move."

He disappears, and Elle makes a noise at my side. "Who's that?"

"My mentor. You didn't sign up for one?"

"No. Clearly I should've."

Beck returns to us through the crowd. "Annie, this is my roommate, Tyler."

It takes a moment to notice the guy at Beck's side. Once I do, my feet root to the floor.

Beck's tall; he's taller. Beck's dark; he's darker. Handsome. Built for sleepless nights and unhealthy obsessions.

There's no blue in Tyler's hair anymore. It's raven black and spiked at the front.

He's wearing fitted jeans, a faded black Henley rolled up at the sleeves. Same tan skin, stubborn chin, but a chest made broader by the years. Ink peeks out from under his shirt sleeve.

This spring, I walked in for auditions and spotted Tyler in a rehearsal room.

The second we locked gazes, my number was called and I took off. Somehow, I got through my audition and even made it in.

I reminded myself Vanier was a big school. We'd probably never even cross paths.

*So much for that.*

Tyler at twenty is different from Tyler at eighteen. If he was handsome before, he's devastating now. It's as if the boy I knew walked off the earth, fought countless battles, and returned a man, vowing never to tell a soul except for the shadows flitting behind his eyes.

He ripped out my heart more than a year ago, but it healed. Maybe it's not the same shape it was, or the same size, but I patched it up with ambition and resolve. There are no cracks in it anymore.

Now...

My chest twinges hard.

Apparently, I missed stitching a spot.

"Hi, Tyler," I say at last.

With a moment's hesitation, he holds out a hand. "Annie."

His voice. I haven't heard his voice in over a year, and it rumbles through me like thunder at a distance, a soft promise of inevitable destruction that will leave no part of me untouched.

I force myself to take his hand.

Beck and Elle have no idea we've met before, and nothing in our greeting would make them suspect.

The heat of him is familiar, but the electricity

traveling from my hand up my arm to my breasts, between my thighs, has me exhaling hard.

His gaze darkens as if he feels it too.

"What are you doing here?" he asks roughly.

"Weird question, bro," Beck says, laughing, but I lift my chin.

"Pursuing the finest arts education money can buy in this beautiful free nation," I say, dropping his hand. "You?"

His gaze narrows. "Same."

"I'm Elle," my new friend volunteers cheerfully. They shake hands, then she turns to my mentor. "You're only second year. Do you really know that much?"

Beck flashes an easy grin. "You know how to score practice rooms during midterms? Get bottomless soda from the vending machine in the library? Hack the staff and faculty meet-and-greet invite list so you can get free booze and mingle with famous alumni?"

She blinks. Even I'm impressed.

"Unofficially, you can be my mentee too," Beck offers generously, stopping to scratch his head. "Wait, isn't that an animal?"

"That's a manatee," Elle says.

His eyes light up. "Right. You can be my manatees. You manatees need anything, you let me know."

"You live in the dorms?" I ask, avoiding Tyler's gaze.

"Nah. They're mostly for first years. We live about a dozen blocks from here, and only the last four are sketchy. Just a booty call away."

"Presumptuous, but I like your style," Elle says. "She's six-oh-six. I'm six-oh-four," she volunteers before I can stop her.

"Six. Got it," Beck continues, and my gut twists sharply as I remember what Tyler used to call me.

"We should get going," I say. "But I'm sure we'll see you around."

"No doubt."

I meet Tyler's gaze again, and reality slams into me.

Of all the issues I thought I'd have in a new city at a new school starting a new part of my life, he wasn't one of them.

But the guy who destroyed me a year and a half ago... he's here. Judging by the fact that he's my mentor's roommate, I'm going to be seeing him.

And judging from the look on Tyler's face, he's as pissed about it as I am.

3

———

# *Annie*

After the assembly, I head to my room to grab my bag for class.

But as I get to the top of the stairs and glance down the hall, I realize my door is ajar. *What the...?*

I push it wide.

Inside is a girl with long, dark hair up in a giant topknot. She has on Beats headphones, and she's brought a backpack and a single trunk that's wedged at the end of the second bed that's been untouched since I moved in yesterday.

"Hey," I volunteer. "I'm Annie. I guess we're roommates."

The girl doesn't answer or take off her headphones but reaches for an earpiece to touch a button.

"Are you Raegan Madani?" I try again. This time, she cuts a glance over her shoulder.

"Rae."

According to the scant roommate info form that included names, contact emails, and majors, she's in contemporary music like me.

Rae opens her backpack, takes out a bunch of tiny figures, and sets them on the top of her headboard. They're little knitted dolls with yarn hair.

Before I can ask, Rae pulls something else out of her bag. "In or out?" she asks.

When I don't respond, she grabs a clean shirt, twists it into a roll, and lays it along the bottom of the door.

My eyes widen as she lights the joint.

"I've heard stories of students getting expelled for less. It would be awesome if you could do that outside."

Rae heaves out a sigh. "Whatever." She grabs her keys off her desk and brushes past me.

*Shit.* I'm not here to make friends, but I don't want to commit social suicide on day one either. From the look Rae tosses me as she heads down the hall, my new roomie might as soon push me in front of a subway as ride it with me.

"Nice meeting you!" I call as I grab my things, then lock up.

With the help of the map on my phone, I find my way on the subway over to the Columbia campus for my first class.

The excitement that's been missing since running into Tyler this morning slowly returns, giving my step extra bounce.

"I haven't seen you since the weekend!" Pen wraps me in her arms when we spot one another outside our lecture hall, and I hug her back. "It sucked we came in on the same flight only to go different directions at the airport," she accuses.

"Gah, I know. I'm sorry."

"Whatever. Gotta pursue your dreams, right? Anyway, glad you made it early so we can grab coffee. There's a café in the same building as our lecture."

We head into the building, and she steers me toward a line of students in front of a counter.

Pen and I scored the same sociology section. I have that, plus English, at Columbia on Tuesday and Thursday. Their campus is only a quick subway ride away, and Vanier has some deal with them so Vanier can focus on arts education while still producing well-rounded grads.

"My clothes don't fit in my room," she goes on. "I might have gone overboard now that we don't have uniforms."

"At least you have a single," I tell her as we order Americanos. "My roommate showed this morning, and I managed to piss her off by telling her to smoke her joint outside."

Pen waves me off. "Etiquette 101. Thou shalt not smoke up in thine dorm room without roommate consent. Or before eleven in the morning because it's tacky."

I sigh. "I missed you."

"Have you talked to your dad and Haley?" she asks as we grab our coffees and head and toward the lecture hall.

"I called them when I got in and texted Dad this morning. Which means I've gone nearly forty-eight hours without blowing cover."

Pen shakes her head. "I still can't believe you didn't tell him about Vanier."

"He wouldn't have let me come. I pitched it to him five times last year. He said if I wanted his support, I would get a real undergraduate degree before deciding whether to, and I quote, 'piss it all away.'"

She drops her bag, settling into a seat. "Daddy J is not the best recruiter for the industry."

"I know he's had issues, but they can't be that bad. Even if they were, he never talks to me about them, so how am I supposed to decide for myself?"

I take the chair next to her.

"There's something else," I say under my breath. "I ran into Tyler Adams this morning."

Pen's nails dig into my arm. "What the hell?"

Heads swivel toward us.

"I told you about seeing him at auditions, but I never thought I'd see him on day one."

Before she can respond, the professor at the front clears his throat. "Welcome to Sociology 101. If you'll take your seats, we can begin."

After a moment of looking torn as the prof talks us through the course outline, my friend pulls her phone from her pocket.

Mine buzzes in my bag a moment later.

**Pen: AND HOW WAS SEEING HIM???**

So many emotions flood me I don't know how to respond.

**Annie: Weird. Horrifying. Exciting. Scary.**

The third word slips out without me meaning to type it.

**Pen: Tell me he grew out of the hot badass look.**

I bite my cheek. Pen's brows rise up her forehead, and she kicks my calf lightly.

**Annie: He grew into it.**

*Maybe you'll see his girlfriend.* I flash back to the girl I saw in his lap the day of auditions, and my gut twists sharply.

She must be a student, too, but she wasn't with him at assembly.

*They could've broken up.*

*Or they could be married.*

It can't matter. Tyler Adams can date whomever he wants.

He left because other things mattered more than me. I should be grateful for the lesson—it taught me to focus on my dreams and not my heart.

This year, I won't fall for anyone. Especially not him.

When class finishes, we pack up and I check my phone. "I have English at one thirty, and you have history. Want to get lunch?"

She lifts a shoulder. "Absolutely. I'm thinking of running for student government, and I need your opinion on my platform. But first, I got you a present."

We head to her dorm, and she opens the door to her single with a flourish. "Behold!"

My gaze lands on the twin goldfish bowls on her desk. "You got us twin fish?"

"Because we might not be at the same school but we'll always be friends."

Gratitude washes over me. "The best."

She grabs me in a hug, then we both turn to study the fish. "What should we call them?"

I cock my head. "Something that speaks to our enduring love. Like... the world may change around us, and we might grow old and die, but we'll always have these fish."

"To be clear, they live five years."

A lightbulb goes on. "I've got it. You want Heathcliff or Cathy?"

Pen snorts with laughter. "Oh my God. You take Heath."

"Deal." I grab one of the fishbowls in my arms, and we head toward the dining hall.

"So, are you going to at least talk to Tyler?" Pen asks once we're outside. "You don't think he'd tell your dad you're here..."

I suck in a shallow breath, adjusting my new pet in my arms. "When Tyler left, he left all of us. Dad would've said something the last year if they'd kept in touch."

"You have to tell your dad eventually."

"I will. But not yet. I need a chance to show him he was wrong about me, and Vanier."

***

By the next morning, I'm learning a few things about my new environment.

One, my roommate appears and disappears at all hours of the night. When I went to bed after hanging out with Pen for most of the day, doing homework in the library at Vanier, and finally meeting Elle and some other girls from our floor for a late dinner, there was no sign of her except for her trunk and dolls in our room.

When I got up to use the bathroom at 4 a.m., Rae was sprawled across her bed, fully clothed down to her white sneakers, and snoring.

By eight, when I get up to shower and dress, she's under the covers.

I catch a glimpse of her schedule printed and lying on her desk and frown. Apparently, she has Entertainment Management Mondays, Wednesdays, and Fridays with me and Elle.

I cross to her bed and prod her shoulder. "You getting up?"

Nothing.

I shrug and head outside to grab Elle for class.

The professor is a young woman who reminds me of Miss Norelli from Oakwood except she's wearing a black blazer over dark jeans.

"In this class, we'll be talking about how to manage a career. The arts aren't only about talent. Plenty of talented people will never pay their bills using those abilities."

"So, once I pull down these silver jeans," Elle says, mimicking the prof's friendly tone from the seat next to mine, "you can practice kissing my ass. A skill that will serve you well in the years to come."

I swallow the laugh and return to taking notes.

I'm most excited for the remaining two classes—my private music lessons, scheduled with my faculty supervisor on Fridays, and my elective.

I chose a studio acting class, which is Wednesdays. I go to class with Elle, where maybe fifteen students are sitting in desks arranged in a semicircle.

The woman at the front has me lifting my brows.

She looks like a librarian, with pale hair twisted up in a knot on her head and a printed floral dress. Her face is wrinkled, but her eyes are sharp beneath her reading glasses.

"Good afternoon, I'm Ms. Talbot. Welcome to my studio intensive. You're all acting students, which means this is what you—yes?" she asks, irritated by my raised hand as I look around.

"I'm in contemporary music, not theater. This is my elective."

Her gaze narrows. "Is anyone else here in contemporary music?"

Two other hands go up—a guy named Jake I met in Entertainment Management and another girl.

"Wonderful. Dilettantes in our midst."

Elle snorts next to me, and she shoots me a "WTF" look as Talbot turns away.

"Today's challenge is as follows," the professor continues. "I will hand you a sheet of paper with a scene on one side and the character's bio on the other. Read the scene without looking at the bio. Your task is to get into your character's head quickly and understand them from their words alone." She points at me. "You want to be here so badly, let's find out why."

I head to the front of the room, squaring my shoulders.

I can do this. I've been in front of far larger crowds. But this feels like my first sort-of performance at Vanier, and it matters.

"I wish you'd listen to me," I read off the sheet she hands me. "I know you think I stand in your way, but I'm not trying to stop you. I'm trying to save you."

A few snickers sound from my classmates looking at the back of my card. I ignore them and go deeper. I feel the pain in the words. Burrow into it as I read.

When I finish the scene, I draw a long breath.

Talbot gestures at my card, and I flip it over.

"Wait—I'm a crossing guard?"

The class bursts into laughter, and my cheeks flame as I go back to my seat.

And it's Elle's turn. She gives a more subtle performance, and I realize this is harder than I figured.

For the last year, all I could think about was coming here, how everything would be solved. Now, as I look at my talented classmates, I realize how far from the truth that is.

"That was brutal," I blurt as we head back upstairs after class, passing a dozen practice rooms, all occupied.

"I've been booed off stage before, so I'm not going to lie to you. It was pretty bad," Elle replies.

"I need to get out of here," I decide as we emerge from the stairwell and head down the hall toward our rooms.

The door to my room is open, and Rae's inside, at her desk on her computer with headphones covering her ears.

"Then let's go out tonight," Elle says, dropping onto my bed as I set my books on my desk. "I saw this place called Leo's that looks cool. They have an open mic night Wednesdays."

"You're gonna need ID."

We both look over in surprise at Rae's voice.

She turns toward us, tugging off the headphones.

"My cousin gave me her old license," Elle says.

Rae crooks a finger, and Elle digs out a driver's license. Rae scoffs. "She's got four inches and thirty pounds on you."

"I'm an actor. It's all about posture." Elle snatches the card back and shoves it in her pocket.

"I don't have ID." I'm sure I could've figured out how to get one, but back home, there weren't clubs close by.

An idea strikes me. *Beck.*

I fire off a text. The response comes almost immediately.

**Beck: Two hours. Fifty bucks. I got you, Manatee.**

After dinner, someone drops off an ID at my door and waits while I get her cash.

I try not to overthink my outfit, deciding on tight black jeans and a matching tank top with my black suede boots. In case it's cold, I throw on a denim shirt overtop.

I twist my hair up in a high bun, then add a hint of mascara, plus some matte red lipstick.

By ten, Elle and I find ourselves outside Leo's.

It's beautiful, industrial, like nothing I've seen back home. Like an old factory with stories to tell.

It's also packed.

"Who is Leo?" I wonder aloud as we wait in line.

"Owner's dead dog," Rae answers.

"Really?" I ask. I'm still surprised she came, but maybe this is a spot of hope.

"No fucking clue." She ducks out of line, and we stare before trailing after her.

Rae stomps up to the door. The bouncer ignores the line of people waiting to glance at our IDs and let us inside.

"How did you do that?" Elle demands of Rae but doesn't get a response.

The inside of the venue is exposed brick, long and skinny, and one story with high ceilings and a stage at one end. The bar's in the center of the room, two thirds of the way from the stage. It's round with a number of bartenders working different sections. The lights behind the bar are old-school theater style, and they spell out "LEO'S" in a burnt-orange glow.

A guy's on stage playing piano, crooning into a microphone. He's good, and I let myself fall into the spell he's weaving.

"You came all the way down here to watch?" Rae tosses at me before disappearing through the crowd.

"You know what?" I call to Elle. "She's right."

I head toward the stage doors, Elle on my heels, and find the woman in charge of the open mic slots.

She looks me up and down, from my tight jeans to my plaid shirt to my ponytail. "We're full."

Dismay works through me as I crane my neck to see her list. "The whole night? Can I at least get on the list for next week?"

"We're full every week. I can't bump one of my regulars for you. Gotta keep this crowd happy."

I bristle, but Elle grabs me and drags me to the bathroom. "She's just putting you off."

Half a dozen other girls compete for sink and mirror space, washing their hands and touching up their careful makeup. Every one of them looks different, but they're all unforgettable.

It's a reminder I've never lived on my own, never truly made my own way.

I'm in a strange city, lying to everyone about where I am and who I am...

*And for what? To drink and watch someone else play music?*

Fear slams into me as I stare into the mirror.

"You done?" an unfamiliar voice demands, jockeying for position.

*You didn't come here to blend in. You survived getting heartbroken, worked your ass off, and now you're here. Don't let them say no.*

The resolve I've built over the past year is a block of iron in my chest, heated by my frustration until it glows red. I strip off my shirt, leaving the tank underneath, and tug out my elastic, fluffing out my hair so it explodes around my head, falling in crazy waves around my shoulders.

I pull out a dark pencil and use it to rim my eyes, top and bottom, until my lashes look even thicker and my eyes pop. Then, I pull out gloss and slick it over my red lips.

"I'm not sure what your plan is," Elle drawls, "but this doesn't go with your outfit."

She unclasps my necklace and hands it to me. I hesitate before dropping it carefully into my purse.

"Thanks. Art is art," I say, turning to inspect myself from the side. "But they need to sell drinks too."

Elle lifts a brow. "You sure you want to do this?"

I take a deep breath. "No."

# 4

# Tyler

"What're we celebrating?" I call over the music as Beck slides a shot down the bar at Leo's.

"Landed an audition." He lifts his glass and clinks mine, and we both drink.

The alcohol burns down my throat, welcome and bracing at once.

The first two days back to school are turning out to be a rude awakening but not for the reasons I expected.

Our fridge is broken, ruining the food I bought on the weekend. Our landlord is dodging me, and the guy I called today to fix it said he'd come by tomorrow between eight and whenever he feels like it.

I had my first weekly guitar lesson this after-noon with my intensive professor—the guy who's assigned to oversee my development—during which he wanted to lecture me about the "evolu-tion of my style."

Which probably could've been avoided if he hadn't insisted on referring to it as the "evolution of my style."

At Leo's, I'm ready to forget all of it for a few hours. A full third of the crowd is from Vanier, but they're here to unwind.

Hell, maybe someone'll catch my eye tonight.

*Because that worked so well the last time.*

"Congrats on the audition," I tell my friend as I set my empty glass on the bar next to his.

He tells me about the new TV series.

"You'd leave school if you got it?"

"Sure. That's what we're all here for."

*Apparently, that's why Annie's here.* I can't stop thinking about her words at the assembly yesterday.

I've thought about what I'd say if I saw Annie Jamieson again, but she caught me off guard, here in the last place I expected, and all I could think was how part of me that'd been dead for a year suddenly woke up.

It took everything in me not to drag her out of that hall to somewhere private and demand she tell me what the hell is going on.

"You ever think about her?" Beck's voice drags me back.

"Who?"

"Meara. She left for LA before the summer. You guys dated."

I shrug. "Not really. We were friends. We went out a few times." She gave me indications of wanting to date, but we both knew the deal—there were more important things than each other.

When she landed a part in LA, I took her to the airport with Beck and some other friends, hugged her, and went on with my day.

We've texted a few times since just to say hey and see how things are going.

"So, that's not why you were brooding all summer."

I stare at him, perplexed. "I wasn't brooding."

"You were, but that means it's not over her. So, it must've been about Zeke."

Beck stares past me, and I follow his gaze to a big poster by the door advertising the annual fall showcase at Vanier.

"You want to get Zeke's attention?" he drawls, grinning. "Close the fall showcase."

I've been so focused on getting my contract back and getting out of Vanier I haven't stopped to think about what to do if I stay this semester.

It's a big deal. Everyone gets written up in the media, and whoever is selected to close gets a ten-grand honorarium.

"It's not the worst idea," I tell him.

"I'm full of 'em today. Really getting into this mentoring thing. My girl's a peach. And cute." My spine stiffens as he continues. "I know you said not to go there, but Ty, you met her. She's fucking adorable. And that voice... I wanna record her saying my name when she comes."

I step closer, my chest tightening. "She's not your girl." The words are out before I can stop them.

His grin turns smug. "She came to me needing something today. I gave it to her."

"What exactly did you give her?"

Before Beck can answer, the sound of applause echoes as performers change.

I glance at the girl taking the stage and freeze an inch from pummeling my roommate.

Even twenty feet from the stage, Annie's dark-rimmed eyes seem to reach straight into my soul.

Her hair's dark and waving over her shoulders. I stopped dying my hair, and she started.

She's wearing high-heeled boots and tight jeans and a shirt—if you can call it a shirt—that pushes up her breasts and stops halfway down her stomach.

My abs clench hard.

I can't decide which part is most responsible for my reaction: the long line of her legs or the soft shadowed dip between her breasts or the slick lips, shiny as if she's been sucking on them.

She looks ripe, like fruit you've been impatiently waiting to soften, telling yourself it's not time yet.

Annie lifts a guitar over her head, and Beck whistles admiringly.

"What do you know? My manatee talked herself into a slot at Leo's. I tell you, Ty, this girl might be it for me."

"Put your dick back in." My quick retort surprises both of us.

The woman on the stage isn't the girl I fell for two years ago. It should be comforting to know that.

Instead, it's disconcerting as hell.

A body bumps mine, a girl blinking at me with apology and thinly veiled invitation. I barely notice, shoving my hands in my pockets as my gaze locks on the stage.

Beck's watching me, though his phone's trained on the stage. "You want her too."

"That's bullshit." I shove both hands through my hair, trying to fight the discomfort clawing at my insides.

"Look at you. You're a mess."

The woman whose hair sways as she bends the strings of the guitar, fingers picking the opening chords of a song, isn't the girl I fell for.

*Which means Annie's gone.*

After leaving Dallas, I consoled myself with the fact that she was still intact somewhere, like a dragonfly in amber—the earnest girl with a disarming smile who'd bleed because that's what we're meant to do.

But she's not, and before I can process the churning in my gut at that realization, the woman on stage starts to sing.

Annie always had the kind of voice you wanted to listen to all day. This is lower, sultrier. It's an invitation and a promise, and it wraps around my spine, drags down.

Annie Jamieson just grabbed my cock in the middle of this bar.

My confusion's gone, squashed by something more deliberate.

The fact that she's here, that she's changed, that she can still turn me on without even touching me, pisses me off.

Beck hollers, and I ignore him, cutting through the half-drunk crowd to backstage.

"Wasn't sure you were coming." The woman who runs open mic night looks at her list. "You want in after her?"

I glance at Annie. "Next one."

I stalk to the edge of the stage. At this new angle, I can see Annie swaying with her own music, the spell she's weaving on the faces of the crowd.

Tightness works through my gut. We're going to talk about this right the fuck now.

How she's here. Why she's here.

*Why the fact that she's here is affecting me so goddamn much.*

My gaze lands on the small silver handbag sitting on an unused speaker. It's familiar, and I reach for it.

When Annie comes off stage, beaming and

sweating from the spotlight, her attention goes to the speaker. "Where's my—"

I hold up the bag, and her eyes flash. When she swipes for the bag, it falls between us, the contents spilling out.

"What are you doing here?" she demands as we both drop to the ground. She reaches for her phone, her face a breath away from mine.

"Leo's is my place. I should be asking you the same thing." I retrieve one of the cards and hold it up in the half light. "It almost looks like you. This you. Whoever she is."

I grab her bag and straighten. She rises too, her gaze lingering on the purse in my hands as if I might run away with it.

"What would your dad say if he could see you like this?" I press.

Annie's close enough I see her breasts heaving under her low-cut top. "I don't care."

I'm not even mad at her. I'm mad at me, at the way she affects me still, at the fact that I left her for my dreams but also so the sweet, smart girl I craved like a drug could grow up without my influence.

But she's not here. That girl is gone.

"Besides," she goes on, "he doesn't know everything that happens in the world."

A single piece in a twisted puzzle clicks into place. "He doesn't know you're here."

There's a hint of panic in those eyes, a vulnerability I catalogue, memorize.

I feel the power shift between us, like I'm suddenly gaining the upper hand.

"Where does he think you are?" I ask.

She looks like she wants to deny me, but there's no point lying. I can find out.

"Columbia."

The next act on stage is playing something down tempo. Now that she's close, I smell her. She's memories and dreams, gold and glory, and parts of me that were dead five minutes ago suddenly ache.

"You shouldn't be so surprised to see me," she goes on. "You saw me at auditions. Couldn't believe I'd actually get in?"

It's my turn to be back on my heels. "I thought I imagined you."

Her brows pull together. "Why would you do that?"

*I don't fucking know. Because I wanted you here?*

"Whatever," she says, realizing I'm not going to answer. "Give my bag back."

I open it and tuck the license back in. When I do, my fingers close on the round glass shape on a chain. I lift it high between us. When the glass flashes in the light, my gut twists.

Hard.

The pendant is flat, cut in the shape of a heart. At first, I think it's purple glass, but when I look closer, I see it's two pieces of clear glass edged with dull gold binding the edges together around the dark-purple thing inside it.

To preserve it.

I can't place it, but familiarity and nostalgia wash over me in uninvited waves.

"What is this?" I demand.

"A reminder that I'm not the person I was. That's the last question of yours I'm going to answer because I don't owe you anything. You walked away from me."

The pain and accusation in her voice has my chest tightening, but I remind myself she's fine. She got over me fast.

"I know Beck's my mentor and he's your roommate," she goes on, "but we can stay out of each other's way."

The way she looks when she says it, the hint of vulnerability in those dark-rimmed eyes, the waver in those gloss-slicked lips, tells me the earnest, honest girl I knew isn't gone. Not entirely.

It makes her ten times harder to ignore.

I steel myself, unwilling to show what I'm feeling as I drop the pendant into the bag and hold it out.

"He likes you," I mutter grudgingly as our hands meet on the fabric.

"Beck?" Her brows lift. "I like him, too."

But her gaze drops down my body before flicking back up. "Don't worry about me. I'm sure your girlfriend is more than enough to keep you occupied."

"My what?"

Doubt has her licking her lips. "The girl who was climbing you in that practice room."

Knowing it bothered her has adrenaline surging through me. I should correct her assumption, tell her Meara wasn't my girlfriend then and isn't now.

But for some fucked-up reason, I need to remind her what went down between us might be over but it happened. More than that, it mattered.

I step closer, inhale her scent as I brush her hair back behind her ear. To her credit, she doesn't back away.

She's all grown up? Fine. I'll treat her like it.

"You want me to pretend I don't know you?" I murmur against her ear. "That I never kissed that mouth? Never slept in your bed?"

*Never made you laugh. Never stared at you in utter awe for how beautiful you were, the way you saw the world.*

I force those thoughts away because they're stirring up feelings I can't stand.

"Never watched those eyes get big when you imagined me fucking you, when you practically begged me to do it?"

The little shiver that overtakes her has me wanting to drop my lips to her jaw, see if it's as soft as I remember.

Applause in the distance tells me the previous performer has wrapped up, and someone shouts at me to take the stage, but I can't move.

She pulls back first, tucking her bag under her arm and sucking in a breath. "That's exactly what I expect. This is my fresh start. No one's going to mess it up. Not even you, Tyler."

As she disappears down the stairs, I don't feel anything like vindicated.

The only thing I can think is that I'd give everything I have to hear her say my name again.

5

———

# *Annie*

"**Y**ou were great at Leo's last night."

I look up from my notebook the next afternoon at the Vanier library to see a slender blond guy from class leaning over my chair.

"Jake," he volunteers. "We survived acting intensive together with Talbot."

"Right." I smile back.

I don't remember seeing him at Leo's, but most of the night I was distracted—by my need to prove myself and by the one guy who could ruin my chances of doing that.

"Homework?" Jake nods to my notebook.

"No, actually. Just writing."

I used to force my brain to work in logic and

answers and solutions. Getting good grades meant everything needed to fit into a cogent argument.

Now, I think in feelings. Emotions.

I don't know if it's an evolution or a devolution.

When I feel something, I drop it onto a page. The words flow out of me, contained by the paper. It keeps them from burning me alive, breaking me from the inside.

"Thanks for the compliment about last night," I say. "It's easy to get lost here there are so many good people."

"I know, right? Did you see that guy, Tyler something? He was the best of the night by far."

I smile tightly. "He was pretty good."

I saw him. He waited for me backstage only to strip me bare with his hard gaze and his harder words. Then I watched him perform, reminding me he's not only the most capable musician but magnetic enough you'd give your soul for another minute in his presence.

*And you practically volunteered that you aren't supposed to be here.*

Chalk it up to being caught off guard. Again.

It's not enough to be in a new place trying to make my way—the one guy from my past has to be holding my secret over my head.

Next time, I'll be ready.

But what the hell was he saying about me getting over him? Did he mean Beck? Is he jealous?

*Impossible.*

"Are you trying out for the fall showcase?" Jake's words have me blinking.

"I heard only upper years get in."

"Doesn't mean you can't try out." His brows wiggle under his hair. "I'm there. Figured you would be, too—you seem like the go-getter type. Auditions are in two weeks, so you better work something up."

He takes off, and I stare after him.

Then I type a message on my phone.

There's a response five minutes later.

**Beck: Meet me in P69.**

It takes me ten minutes to figure out P refers to the practice rooms, not parking, but there's no 69.

It takes me another five minutes to find the closed door with a small window and P69 carved into the door.

I knock on the door, and it opens an inch.

Inside, Beck's sitting in a desk chair, feet propped on a shelf.

"What is this place?" I ask. "It looks like a supply closet."

"Practice rooms are hard to come by. Sometimes you gotta grab whatever you can find."

He pulls the door open, and I wedge myself inside.

"What're you working on?" I look at his computer and the book in front of him.

"*King Lear*. And my vlog." He nods at his computer. "New episode every week."

I glance as his profile, my brows lifting. "That's a lot of subscribers."

"Half wanna watch me strip. Half are actually interested in what I have to say." He cocks his head. "But you wanted to hear about the showcase. It's the BFD. You want to get noticed in this city, that's how you do it. The biggest casting agents, producers, directors—everyone comes. You see the EGOT wall downstairs?"

I think of the portraits in the main hall. "Hasn't everybody?"

"All of 'em not only played the showcase but closed it. And I happen to know who's gonna close this year." He grins.

Electricity hums through my body. "You mean your roommate."

Beck shrugs. "The guy's a beast with a guitar. Everyone thinks it's going to be his year."

"What do you think?" I ask.

He shifts back in his chair, braces one foot on the table he's rigged up as a desk. "I might be more Shaw and Shakespeare than Stryker or the Stones, but even I can tell that dude's gonna burn up a stage. And my roomie needs a break. Be patient. You'll have your shot next year."

"It's supposed to be an open competition, Beck. Are you afraid I'll take it from him?"

He smirks, appreciation flashing in his eyes. "I'm not worried about you beating him head to head. I'm worried about you messing with his head." Surprise slams into me as he continues. "I saw you at Leo's. You were good. Thing is, it wasn't nearly as interesting as watching my roommate watch you."

I fold my arms across my chest. "I don't know what that means."

"Doesn't matter. What I'm saying is Ty's been through some shit and if anyone deserves a break, it's him."

Surprise washes over me. "Why? What happened to him?"

"Not my place to say. But he's good people, Manatee. The best people."

An ache forms low in my gut. "Here. At least let me move this box. You'll have more room."

He shifts over an inch, and I manage to pry a box of nails off the floor and stick them onto a shelf. When I look up, Beck's watching me.

"You think working your ass off in a supply closet isn't glamorous," he guesses. "But it is, because here's the secret."

He crooks a finger, and I humor him, leaning in.

"They *all* wanna be us. We're the rebels, Manatee. The jerks at Harvard on track to their corner offices or lining up for eighteen-hour-a-day internships on Wall Street—in thirty years, they'll look up from their fake wood desks to the fake gold clock on the fake stone mantle and think, 'What if?'"

The words are still ringing in my head when I leave.

My phone buzzes on my way back through the halls, heading for the stairwell that afternoon. I answer, dread filling my stomach.

"Hey. What's up?"

Dad says, "There you are. I was starting to think I'd have to get on a plane to talk to you." I feel the blood drain from my face before he continues. "How are your classes?"

"Good." I tell him about sociology and English, which I can be truthful about. "I'm still waiting on one that I have tomorrow." My intensive professor, whom I haven't had the chance to meet, is supposed to see me then.

I reach for the stairwell door, both to avoid the traffic in the elevators and because the reception's probably better.

"I know you were disappointed when I said you couldn't go to performing arts school." His gruff voice has my stomach twisting with guilt. "But I wanted to say... you're the first one in our family to get a real college degree. And Columbia's nothing to shit on."

Lying to my dad sucks, but I have to do it for a while.

After all the music classes I took, I deserve to be here. Dad telling me he'd pay for any degree except performing arts was bullshit. He even said he'd pay for me to travel for a year if that's what I wanted.

But there was only one place I wanted to go.

New York.

Last winter, after I finished a local theater production of *Avenue Q* and before the start of Oakwood's spring musical, I decided I didn't need permission.

I'm following my dreams. When he sees me succeed, he'll understand. I know he will.

I just need a little time to figure out how to show him I'm right.

"How's Sophie?" I ask as I reach the sixth floor, panting, and make my way down the hall to my room. "And Haley?"

"Sophie's a monster. Haley's not much better."

"Heard that."

I smile at the sound of my stepmom's voice as I stop in front of my closed door.

"House is quiet without you," he says after a minute.

"You're not even in the house. I thought you were lobbying in Washington this week."

"We are. But it'll be quiet when we get home. What do you need? Money? Clothes?"

"I'm fine. Thanks." I slide my key into the lock and turn the handle.

"Okay. Guess I'll let you go. Oh, and don't forget about that awards dinner."

"What awards dinner?"

"We talked about it months ago. The flight's booked. I sent you an email about it this morning."

*Shit.* I almost forgot my dad was being honored at this big thing in LA Friday night and having a smaller friends and family thing at home Saturday. "Right. I'm sorry. I really want to come, but school's just started. It's hard to leave."

"Annie. It's two days. You won't miss any classes. The band's planning to come down, plus Lita and Nina if they're around."

I squeeze my eyes shut at the thought of all his crew, basically my adopted family. "All right. Sure."

"Good. We love you, kid."

"Love you too, Dad. And tell Sophie I miss her." My throat works as I hang up.

Before I can push my door in, the door next to mine opens.

"That sounded strained." Elle leans against the doorjamb, nodding at my phone. "Your parents?"

"My dad," I admit. "I need a way to show him coming to Vanier was the right decision."

As I say the words, a lightbulb goes off.

There's no sign of Rae as I go to my computer and print something off.

"Fall showcase?" Elle scoffs when I stick the poster over my bed.

"I'm going to get in. No," I decide, "I'm going to close."

Her brows hit her hairline. "You have any idea how you're going to execute this coup?"

"Not yet," I admit. "But I'll figure it out. I didn't come all this way for nothing."

I glance at Rae's bed, the shelf over the headboard. "Wait, weren't there more of those dolls?"

Elle crosses the room, inspecting the shelf. "You're right. There was one with hair just like yours. She asked to borrow my scissors too…"

I stare her down. "Okay, you're shitting me."

With the exception of Leo's last night, when Rae disappeared and was still gone when Elle and I returned to the dorms, I've barely seen her.

"I don't think she's planning to voodoo you in your sleep."

"Ugh. I'm not so sure." I drop onto my bed and clutch the stuffed Flounder Haley got me after *The Little Mermaid*. It's a bittersweet reminder of home.

Elle's face appears over mine. "You've never had someone not like you before?"

"Yes, but…" I'd always figured it was because I was Jax Jamieson's daughter and I didn't meet what they expected of me. "Not someone who shares my towel rack."

Elle laughs, dropping down onto the bed next to me.

"What's so funny?" I demand.

"You think people liking you or not is about you? It's about them. Let me guess—you have a lot of damage."

"A lifetime's worth in eighteen years," I confirm.

She nods. "Now imagine everyone in this entire place is walking around with the same damage." My brows shoot up, but she holds up a hand. "For every scar you've got, every mean girl story, every 'daddy hates me' and 'I'm not enough' and 'it should've been different'"—my chest tightens at how scarily accurate she is—"they have one too. So does Rae. I promise you."

I turn that over. "You seem reasonably unscathed."

Elle smiles, pointing to her face. "It's the brows.

You keep your eyebrow game on point, the world thinks you have your shit together."

I huff out a breath as I stroke Flounder's blue-and-yellow fur, thinking of Oakwood. "I'm not the best at making new friends."

"Because you're into voodoo too?"

I throw the fish at her head, and she catches it, laughing.

She looks between the stuffed fish and the goldfish bowl on the corner of my desk. "I've heard of a foot fetish. A fish fetish is new. I might have to use that."

"That's Heath."

"Heath," she echoes.

"Heathcliff. As in *Wuthering Heights*." My chest warms a little as I watch him blow his introspective little bubbles. "He's from my friend Pen. She's at Columbia."

"Ahh. So, you do have friends."

I roll my eyes. "Some."

"Well, I've got your back. Rae can do what she wants."

A smile tugs at my lips. "Thanks."

My gaze settles on the trunk at the foot of Rae's bed, which I've yet to see her open. "Is it wrong to want a hint of her damage?"

We look at the trunk, then each other.

Elle runs her hand over the surface of the trunk, landing on the lock at the front. "Until last night when you stripped off all your clothes to get on stage, I had you pegged as a good girl."

"I was. I grew up."

She lifts a brow. "Doesn't that mean the end of childish ways?"

"No. It means accepting that we all do bad things for good reasons."

# 6

# Tyler

New York produces the kind of cold that gets into your bones and won't leave.

Today, New Yorkers brace against the fall wind with flipped collars on coats.

I'm one of them as I get my motorcycle from the tiny spot I sublet for cheap in a parking garage around the corner.

Then I head to a studio in Brooklyn to win my contract back.

"Zeke around?" I ask at the front desk.

"Not today," the woman informs me with a half smile. "You're in studio two."

I brush off my disappointment as I head to the assigned studio. Inside, I shake hands with the band. As I get out my guitar and take a seat on the stool to tune it, the singer approaches me.

"We made some changes to the first track and added a couple new ones since we reached out to you." He passes me his notes. "You need a minute to take a look?"

I scan the sheet. "No."

"You sure?"

I calmly look at him, then play the section with the changes. "We can do it like that. Or—" I redo it with some flourishes that elevate it. "Like that."

He claps a hand on my shoulder, grinning. "Let's keep it simple."

When I came to New York last summer and signed with Zeke, I had a chance to be the one calling the shots. I fucked it up.

Jax wanted me to walk away from Annie and from Dallas so I could do something great.

I tried to throw myself into it, but right when I thought I was done with my father, he played one last card that pulled me away from the city and from my new gig for two weeks.

By the time I got back to New York, I'd missed deadlines, messed with schedules, and generally had Zeke cursing out my name loudly enough to be heard in Jersey.

He put me out on my ass.

Getting into Vanier through a connection was grace in the highest sense.

The throng of students who were all like me—I'd never been around people who *wanted* so fucking much—grounded me. Piece by piece, I rebuilt myself and tried to put it behind me.

Beck helped, and so did my music.

Even though I'm not where I expected, I'm a better musician than I was last year.

But it wasn't until a girl who looked like Annie Jamieson walked through the halls last April—of course it was her, but at the time, I swore I was hallucinating—that I pounded on Zeke's door again, demanding he revisit our arrangement.

He "declined." A nice way of saying "Fuck off." I didn't stop calling, and within weeks, I was offered my first session gig.

Today, we spend four hours running the tracks on the list. I do as I'm told, even lose myself in it once or twice.

Before I can leave, the producer calls me over. "Appreciate the help with this. I have another gig for you next week. You interested?"

Yes, I'm interested, but I want to say, *This isn't the work I pictured. I want more. I'm better than this.*

"I'll check my calendar," I say at last.

After heading back to our place and making my way back to our building from the parking garage, I come across my roommate smoking a joint outside.

"Guy never came to fix the fridge," he says tonelessly.

"I'll call him. How was the audition?"

Beck holds out the joint, and I shake my head. "I'm not getting a callback. I was fucking De Niro in there," he says with a wry grin. "But when I left, there were a dozen guys who looked exactly like me lining the hall. Stopped at the lobby vending machine for a Coke, and there was a guy who just had his change eaten who was shaking it. He even sounded like me. If that's all there is to look forward to, what're we even doing this for?"

As I take in his expression, I feel a pang of empathy.

Beck's good at what he does, and it's still an uphill climb every day just to get a chance at a dream.

If I was smart, I'd line up session jobs, string 'em together to make for enough paydays, but it's not enough.

The life I once told myself I wanted is within

my grasp, but I'm restless. Maybe the thing Vanier's helped me realize is that I want to create something that's mine, that no one can take from me.

"It's almost your birthday," I remind him. "Twenty'll be good, Beck. More auditions, more gigs, more pretty boys giving you pretty blowjobs."

"Fuck it. I'm gonna curl up under the covers until someone notices I'm gone."

"I'll notice."

He gives me side-eye. "Not once the fridge is fixed."

I bark out a laugh, and he offers me the joint again. This time, I take it, but mostly for an excuse to stay with him.

"You heard from your parents since the party last weekend?" I ask.

He shakes his head. "Nah. We always used to go to this restaurant for my birthday. Get a private room. Hell, last year I even started to think my parents were coming around to the acting thing. My mom beamed when I told her about my Shakespeare in the Park gig. My dad told me about this guy he replaced two valves on who was a big ex-producer from Hollywood." His eyes glaze. "Between the entrée and dessert, the prettiest waiter showed me his cock in the bathroom. It was a good birthday, man."

Something tells me that's not happening this year. Beck's always been a good friend, but with coming out to his family and his upcoming birthday and this bad audition news...

I need to up my roommate game.

---

Normally, I'm a hundred percent confident walking around Vanier. But sometime between my genius idea yesterday and this morning, I've realized this is a terrible idea.

*Fuck it. This is for Beck.*

I take the elevator at Vanier and knock on the cracked-open door of six-oh-six at the end of the hall.

There's no answer, but I slowly push it open to reveal a girl with straw-blond hair and alert eyes perched in a chair by one of the two desks.

"I'm looking for Annie," I say.

"She's in the bathroom."

"I'll wait." I realize she's the girl who was with Annie at the opening assembly, the one who said she was in six-oh-four. "Elle, right? This isn't your room."

"Not yours either."

She's got me there.

But Elle returns to a notebook computer, and I step inside.

I know immediately which half of the room is Annie's. The cover on the bed is purple, and there's a stuffed fish on the pillow.

Fish on the desk, too. Huh.

"Working on something for class?" I ask, mostly to make small talk.

"New bits for a set. I'm a comic."

I shoot her an admiring look. "That's thankless."

"I get off on being laughed at. Tried eight years of therapy and learned this is cheaper."

A standard-issue dresser draws my gaze. There are photos on top and a frame turned down. I lift it to find a picture of Annie with Jax, though he's wearing sunglasses and a grin and is almost unrecognizable.

I set the picture right-side up.

Under it is a stack of Polaroids.

It takes me a second to realize what they are. Words in black ink on an organic canvas.

My tongue wets my lip, and I glance over my shoulder to where Elle's typing on her keyboard.

I read the lines on the first picture, absorb them into my soul before turning carefully to the next. There're a couple of dozen photos. I get through half before a sound drifts into my brain.

"What are you doing?"

The sharp voice has me turning.

Annie's standing at the door, and my gaze drags down her body—her toes, painted the same purple as her bed; long, curvy legs; the dip between her breasts just above the top of a knotted towel; the long hair, darkened and piled on top of her head, a few strands dripping on her bare shoulders; that oval face, full lips and amber eyes brimming with accusation.

Desire slams into me, but I manage to slide the photos behind my back.

"Elle?" Annie demands before I can respond, but Elle looks between us, eyes narrowing in fascination.

"You have a gentleman caller," she drawls.

Annie folds her arms over her chest. "Tyler's no gentleman. Why are you here?"

I force my attention to her face. "I need your help. The other night you... asked me for something." From the way Annie sucks in a breath, she gets I'm talking about keeping her secrets. "I want something from you, too."

"Elle—" Annie starts, and I hold up a hand.

"It's fine," I say. "She can stay."

"Why, thank you." Elle grins, shifting back in her seat to study us as if we're two different species trying to mate.

I turn back to Annie. "Beck had this audition he's been psyched for all week. It didn't go well. He's also had some shit going on, and it's his birthday this weekend. Maybe we can do a little party or a cake? The kind that doesn't need refrigerating," I amend.

Her suspicion is replaced by concern, and if I wasn't sure she cared about him, I am now.

Annie sits on the bed, crossing her legs. The towel rides up, and I press my tongue against the floor of my mouth to keep from swallowing it.

"Beck needs a party," she says.

"We could take him to a club," Elle volunteers.

"Like Leo's?" I ask.

Annie shakes her head slowly. "No. Somewhere you can dance."

Elle leaps up and snaps her laptop closed. "I'm in. I want to dance my ass off. Hell, I bet even Rae would come. Sure, she'd cross the street to avoid us, but the girl likes to party."

Annie cocks her head at Elle. "Where're you going?"

"Funeral. I don't know the guy," she says as she reaches for the door. "They're the only place to witness the full range of human emotions. And they usually have snacks."

In a moment, Elle's gone, leaving Annie and me in a room that somehow feels smaller than it did with three of us in it.

"Your neighbor goes to strangers' funerals and your roommate avoids you," I say. "Nice girls."

"I'm pretty sure Rae's going to voodoo me out of Vanier."

I cross to the bed with the little figures along the back and bend to look at them. "They don't look sinister."

We exchange a smile that's gone as fast as it appears, as if we've both realized it's an old habit, and a bad one at that.

"I need to get dressed," she says, watching me with an unreadable expression. "I have class."

She's already opening a drawer, pulling out clothes. I turn away, the photos still in my hands.

The unmistakeable whoosh of a towel dropping has my head jerking upright.

*Is she naked right now?*

"I'm auditioning for the fall showcase," Annie says from behind me, forcing me to focus on her words instead of wondering what color panties she's pulling on. "Beck says I shouldn't because you need it more."

The rise and fall of her voice says she's moving, but I can't hear any clothes.

"You didn't need it last year. You had an offer to work for Zeke. So, how'd you end up at Vanier?"

My chest tightens. I'd rather be tortured by her undressing behind me than talk about this, but I force out a response. "The contract didn't work out."

"Why not?"

I thumb through the photos in my hands, a dull ache in my chest. "It doesn't matter. Life is hard. We have to go after what we want."

"Like you did."

Pain rips through my gut. "I thought I was doing the right thing. For everyone, Six."

I didn't mean to blurt out the nickname, but I can't take it back.

In that instant, I'm remembering the time I went to see her, two months after I left Dallas.

It was after the shit with my dad and with Zeke.

I rode all night to get to there because I needed to see her, to know something in this world made sense.

She had no idea I was there, sitting on my bike, the ache of weeks of not sleeping and hours of riding heavy in my bones.

I wanted to tell her I'd fucked up—not because I lost my contract, but because I missed her and I hated that I couldn't text her funny things from my day, that I didn't get to hear her low voice in my ear... that I didn't get to kiss her, to feel her breath mix with mine.

I wanted to say Jax was wrong, that I'd be willing to do whatever it took to be the guy she needed.

I hadn't thought of what would happen when I got to her, just that when I did, everything would somehow be okay.

It wasn't. At least, it wasn't the okay I expected.

She was standing outside the library where she was working for the summer with a guy—not someone from Oakwood, or I would've known him. She was smiling and laughing, and without so much as looking at me, it was clear that we were done. She was over it.

I had to be over it too.

When she responds, her voice is lower, more vulnerable. "If you'd told me you chose your career over me, I would've understood. But you just left. I know it was high school, but one second you were sleeping next to me and kissing me and touching me, and the next you were gone. Did I do something to fuck it up?"

"No. Never."

The ache is more than physical now, as if it's pulling at the corners of my soul. Talking to each other without seeing each other feels safe, as if there are no stakes, no rules—as if every word is no sooner spoken than forgotten.

I drop my head back, shutting my eyes and remembering that day, seeing her with that guy. "You got over me," I say, needing confirmation.

"I wrote you sixty-three times. Emails, texts, letters. All summer, halfway through the fall." Her low laugh is dry. "I didn't send them, didn't try to reach you, because I didn't want to be selfish. I knew you chose your future, and that was enough for me."

The anguish rips through me, and I force myself to stop tearing at the edges of the Polaroids in my fingers. The backs of my eyes burn, and I swallow against the emotion rising up my throat.

"It wasn't enough." My voice comes out rough. "You taught me to want things I never let myself want. Fuck, Annie. You taught me to dream."

Her shallow intake of breath has me turning, and once I do, I can't look away.

Here, in a black bra and panties with wet hair sliding over her shoulders, she's more than a dream.

My gaze drags down her small breasts, her stomach, the flare of her hips.

I can't remember a time when I wasn't attracted to her, but now she's every wish and regret and ache wrapped into a single person.

I was a boy who cared too much. She was a girl infatuated with something she didn't understand.

None of that's responsible for the way the air crackles between us *now*, for the way her eyes widen in warning as if she feels it too.

"Tyler..."

I close the distance between us, one slow step at a time. When I come to a stop inches away from her, the blood pounds in my veins, my ears, my temples.

"Give those back."

Her voice has an edge it didn't a moment ago, and I blink when I realize her gaze has dropped to my hands—to what I've forgotten to conceal.

She lunges for the photos, and I hold them out of reach.

When her half-naked body brushes my chest through my T-shirt, she's close enough I can smell her light floral scent, and I want to drop the photos and tangle my fingers in her hair, drag her angry mouth to mine.

As if maybe that can fix what's between us, what's inside each of us.

"You wrote them about me." My voice is a rasp, and her chin snaps up, eyes flashing.

"Taylor Swift writes a song after every breakup. Doesn't give her exes the right to hear her private thoughts until she makes them public."

Her breath is light on my face, her lips close enough I could swoop down and claim them, learn whether her taste is the same or whether it's changed, too.

"One problem with that assessment." I breathe, and her brows lift. "We never dated."

She shoves against my chest. I don't budge, but I do capture her hand with one of mine, hold it there until she stops trying to twist away.

"I don't care what you call it," she retorts. "I was a kid. I was in…"

"In what?" Her palm covers my heart, and I know she can feel it hammer in my chest.

We stare each other down, neither of us ready to give in.

I want her to finish that sentence more than I've ever wanted anything, as if her saying she loved me gives permission for me to unload on her, too.

To tell her she was my entire damned world, that when I learned she was at Vanier, I was confused and frustrated, but more than all of it?

I was fucking elated.

The one thing I consoled myself with a year ago was that she'd be better off without me. I never let myself use the L-word with her, swore that whatever I felt for her was mixed up shit amplified by our circumstances.

*You can't fall in a matter of weeks.*

*Just like you can't fall for someone who's not talking to you.*

*Who refuses to look your way in the hall.*

*And she can't fall for you.*

I was wrong. I see it now.

But even if she didn't get over me as fast as I thought, even if there's still enough attraction between us to incinerate a city...

She's over me now. I know it when she pulls her hand out from under mine, and my blood cools a degree the second her touch is gone.

"The photos, Tyler."

I hand her the stack. Annie turns and sets it on her dresser under the photo of her and her dad.

Then she grabs the faded jeans on her bed and tugs them on. I don't bother looking away. She doesn't ask me to.

The desire's still there, but it's overshadowed by something bigger, an uninvited emotion filling my chest.

"So, if I help you throw this party for Beck tomorrow night, you'll keep my secrets," she says under her breath.

"I will."

Annie buttons her jeans, straightening to look me dead in the eye. "Tomorrow, then. For Beck."

I nod. "For Beck."

But as I start for the door and she turns away to

reach for a shirt, my gaze drags back to the stack of photos...

Hating that I didn't realize how deeply I'd hurt her.

Wondering what parts of her body she inked me on.

Wishing she'd never erased me.

**7**

---

# *Annie*

"How nervous are you?" Elle asks me on the way out of Entertainment Management Friday.

"It's going to be great. I didn't even know Finn was on the faculty list until the fall," I admit as we start down the hall. "He wasn't when I auditioned."

"Finn Harvey?"

I look up to see Jake, the guy from the library, fall into step with us.

"Lucky," he goes on. "The guy's a rising star. But I don't know anyone else who got Finn. It'll be cool to work with someone who knows how to bust in."

Excitement works through me. "Exactly."

Elle jerks her head toward the dining hall. "I'm

this way. Annie, I'll catch you tonight?" Her eyebrows wiggle.

"For sure."

"What's tonight?" Jake prompts as she leaves.

"A bunch of us are going out to this club. You should come." I give him the details, and he nods.

"You give any thought to the showcase?" he prompts.

"Yeah. I'm auditioning for sure." Last night I watched some video from past events. The talent level is off the charts, particularly from the people who close.

But the faculty who preside over the auditions have to choose someone. I'm already strategizing how to make sure that someone is me.

"It'll be a first-year uprising." Jake pumps a fist in the air giddily.

I wave goodbye, then head for the stairs to the practice rooms on the second floor. I'm five minutes early, and my swipe card doesn't let me in. I wait in the hallway, watching people flow by.

Classes have been tough the first week, but deciding to focus on the showcase has given me an anchor, a reminder of why I'm here.

I'll do whatever it takes to be that good. No excuses, no distractions.

Tyler coming to my room yesterday was a distraction.

Not only walking in to find him there, studying my things as if he had every right to be in my space, but the things he said...

*"You taught me to want things I never let myself want. You taught me to dream."*

And the look on his face—like I was the most beautiful thing he'd ever seen.

It doesn't matter that he sounds torn up about what happened between us. He's the one who walked away.

My hand finds my necklace under my shirt.

After *The Little Mermaid*, I took the rose Tyler had handed me in the garden and had it preserved in order to remember what happened, to remind myself I'm not fragile and that my dreams matter more than a broken heart.

Now, every time I look at it, I think of him.

I'm not letting him in again. We can coexist, we can even be civil, but we're not going to be friends. We're definitely not going to be more than that.

I'll have my chance to practice keeping him out because we're all going out to a club tonight for Beck's birthday.

"You ready?"

My gaze snaps up as a guy maybe ten years older than me appears down the hall dressed in jeans and a denim jacket over a dark T-shirt. His hair is dirty blond and unruly, as if the wind had its way with it.

"Finn. Mr. Harvey? I'm Annie. It's nice to meet you."

"Finn's good." He retrieves something from his pocket and waves it in front of the door.

The door unlocks, and I follow him inside.

I set my bag on the floor. "How did you end up at Vanier?" I ask.

"They've got a push on recruiting people with industry experience for the contemporary program. An old friend twisted my arm."

The room is about half the size of my dorm room upstairs, and it contains a piano with a bench, three stools, a white board, and two music stands.

Finn says, "So, the next semester of lessons is supposed to improve your technique and performance, blah, blah, blah. But none of that can happen unless I know why you're doing this. So, tell me what you want."

His bluntness has me leaning in. "I want to be on a stage."

"Why?"

I blink. "Because I love creating music. I love when I'm in it."

"Why else?"

I dig deeper, thinking of what drove me to work my ass off these past couple of years.

"Because I want the world to see me."

Satisfaction works across his expression. "Show me."

I take a seat at the piano and play my audition piece, singing overtop.

He cuts me off three bars in. "No."

I try something else. And another. And another.

Each time, he stops me. "Any kid in a talent contest could sing that."

"Then tell me what you want me to sing," I say eventually, frustrated. I rise from the piano bench and turn to face him. "I have some classical training, but I can't give you Puccini or Strauss. Maybe someone in the next room can"—I hitch a thumb at the wall—"but this is what I am."

He's standing in the corner, smirking. "I wouldn't be wasting my time here for Puccini or Strauss. I saw your audition tape. You grabbed me. You want to be seen, make me see you."

My chest tightens. Moments before the audition, I'd run into Tyler. It was a kick in the gut. It took everything I had to make it through my piece. I was raw and desperate and earnest.

*I don't know how to be that girl again.*

My fingers find my necklace again, twisting the chain between my fingers. Under Finn's stare, I think of the pictures Tyler found in my room, the words I wrote when I was coming apart.

I reach for the fallboard and tug it down over the piano keys. Then I shift back onto it, perched on the edge, resting my feet on the bench.

"A heart breaking has multiple acts. It doesn't break in a moment; it breaks over years.

"It tears, not in half, not perfectly. But in layers. Like flower petals.

"Pieces, one at a time. Peeling away.

"And you can put it back together. Collect the pieces. Sew them back.

"It might even look the same, from the outside."

I lift my gaze to see Finn leaning against the opposite wall, his face impassive.

My throat tightens, and I force myself to take a breath that fills my lungs even though it's hard.

He's going to tell me it's not a song.

He's going to kick me out, say this was all a mistake, that he doesn't want to supervise me.

He doesn't.

Instead, he says, "Keep going."

---

"Are we having fun yet?" Elle asks over the music, reacting to my grin as I dance next to her.

"Better than class," I call back.

I've never been to a bar or club except for a concert. This place, with its pounding bass and neon lights and grinding bodies, barely seems in the same category as Leo's.

If the first few days were like learning to play an impossible sheet of music, the rest of week one was like turning the page and realizing there are ten more pages, each harder than the last.

After my lesson with Finn, which improved somewhat in the last fifteen minutes in that he let me finish but still said we had a lot of work ahead of us, I started sociology homework only to realize I've been working from an old textbook.

Wednesday, Talbot assigned us hours of film to watch before next week's class, which is going to be nearly impossible given I'm going to Dallas for the weekend for my dad's celebration. Plus, I narrowly avoided slipping up on the phone when we were talking about my visit.

*Once I get the showcase, everything will be okay.* I repeat it like a mantra.

Auditions are in three weeks. I need to use every second I have to choose the right piece, to work it until it's perfect.

But for tonight, it's hard not to want to let loose and be young and alive.

"You seen Jake?" I ask Elle. "He said he'd come tonight."

He's the only first year who seems to want the showcase as much as I do.

Elle shakes her head. "But there's Rae!"

She points at the DJ booth, where Rae's charmed her way in.

I'm no closer to making inroads with her. I know she makes electronic music. Her chest has an old-style turntable and a bunch of mixing equipment. But I don't know about her family or her dreams or anything except what toothpaste she uses.

My phone vibrates in my bag.

Beck: **BAR. NOW.**

Elle and I wind through the crowd to where Beck is holding court at the bar in a pale-purple dress shirt, half tucked-in. His dark hair is spiked, his grin wide.

"Shots!" he demands.

The bartender's pouring into almost a dozen glasses, and I wrinkle my nose.

Beck passes me two, and I pass one back. "Going home for the weekend tomorrow," I tell him.

He slides back the second shot. "Your family's anything like mine, this might help."

I grin as my attention skims the group of us at the bar—about ten from Vanier, a mix of first years we know and second years Tyler invited—my gaze locking on a familiar one a few bodies away.

Tyler's a dark knight all in black. His dress shirt is rolled at the sleeves, revealing curls of ink that trace one arm like venom taking over his bloodstream.

A wave of desire washes over me before I can stop it. Electricity buzzes through me—my lips, my fingers, my bare shoulders and breasts under the backless silver halter top I bought this afternoon.

Dammit, I want to know what happened when he came to New York.

I want to know what he's thinking right now.

*Stop wondering.*

I toss back the drink. The sweetness and alcohol burn down my throat, settling in my stomach with a not unpleasant buzz.

The next second, Elle's between us, an expression of shock on her face.

"Jake isn't coming. He got kicked out of school today. He was selling uppers from his dorm room."

The comfortable warmth of the booze is overtaken by disbelief. "It's the first week of school." I look between Elle and Beck.

Beck shrugs. "Sometimes you want something so bad you'll give up who you are to get it."

My chest feels hollow.

Yes, Jake fucked up, and I won't do that, but you can be on top one moment and back on the bottom the next.

"You know what time it is, Manatee?" Beck proclaims, and I try to refocus on him. "It's dancing time."

"I'll be right there. Think I need that second drink after all."

I watch him and Elle head toward the floor.

When I reach for the second shot, fingers close around my wrist.

I jerk my head up to see Tyler looming over me, holding a plastic cup of what looks like water.

"I don't want it," I say.

"What do you want?"

I lift my chin, suddenly angry. "I want people to stop leaving. Everyone leaves."

I pry the shot from his hand and down it before taking off toward the dance floor.

I'd thought once I got to Vanier the rest would be easy. None of it's easy.

Once I find my friends, I link hands with Elle and Beck, and the three of us dance.

I focus on the music.

That's what I've always wanted—to lose myself in its power, to be part of it.

Elle splits off to dance with a guy from school, and Beck grins at me.

I move closer. My hand finds his shoulder, and he smiles.

"This is a good birthday, Manatee. But I'm supposed to be helping you, not the other way around."

My chest expands. "We're friends, right?"

He nods. "For sure."

The song changes to something hip-hop, and

when his hands find my hips, I go with it, moving closer.

My arms wind around his neck as I smile up at him.

Beck cuts a look past me, looking bemused. "Fascinating."

"What is?"

"What's gonna happen in five, four, three, two…"

Someone brushes my back, and Beck angles his head up, hands not moving from my body. "Hey, man."

Tyler says something to his friend I can't hear.

"Girl needed some mentoring, if you know what I mean." Beck winks at me, and I laugh in response.

But Tyler's back at his ear, and Beck's smile dims.

Before I can react, Beck lifts my hand, presses his lips to the back in a move that's somehow cheesy and earnest at once. "Thanks for the dance."

A little tingle runs through me, and I bite my cheek as I watch him head back through the crowd.

"What did you say to him?" I demand, whirling to face Tyler.

"He's not for you." He's a foot away, a muscle leaping in his jaw.

Everything from this week piles on top of itself until I'm feeling as if I'm in a different dimension than the carefree dancing people around me. "You don't know that."

"You're already hanging with the brother of your stepmom's best friend when you're hiding out here. You're gonna fuck him too?"

I blink up at him, trying to make sense of the meaning behind his frustrated words.

*Beck.* Serena's Beck, the one she mentioned had gotten into Vanier...

"No." They have different last names, but it's too much of a coincidence.

His gaze narrows, and I know it's true.

"Does he know who I am?" I manage.

"He hasn't put it together. But he will. Who knows? Maybe if you hook up with him, he'll keep your secret."

Someone bumps me from behind, and I step forward. Tyler's hands are there, catching me by the arm and the waist.

"You didn't used to be such a prick," I state, angry.

"You didn't used to be such a flirt. He can't make you happy."

His words catch me off guard. "Why not?"

"Because you need someone who understands what makes you tick, like those music boxes you used to collect. Someone who knows you're going to get into trouble, who has your back when you do."

I could pull away, but there's barely enough room to breathe. "And that's you?"

Tyler bends closer, his lips near my ear so suddenly I can't stop him. "It's not him."

The truth of those words hangs between us.

Since I moved here, it feels as if this new world is a dark, vast ocean dotted with sharks under the water.

Tyler is familiar—a beacon in its own treacherous tide but one I know.

All I want is a night to forget that I'm alone in this city, that people rise and fall in an instant, that the only boy I ever loved has moved on and so have I.

The song changes again, a sexy downtempo remix of "Pretty Young Thing."

I turn but don't step away. My shoulders bump his chest, my ass hitting his thighs. I roll my body once, twice. The friction of his clothes on my ass, the bare skin of my back, makes me bite my lip.

He doesn't move.

Catching Tyler by surprise is reward enough, but I push my luck.

I reach up behind my head for his neck, brush the edge of his hair above his collar. My fingertips trail along his scalp.

Tyler responds so fast it makes my breath hitch.

He drags me closer with strong arms. His hand splays across my stomach, and when his thumb slips under the edge of my shirt, his pinkie under the top of my skirt, he hardens against my back.

*Fuck.* I wonder if I'm tall enough to ride this ride.

But I'm more than capable of handling Tyler Adams.

So, I lean my head back against his chest and close my eyes.

The bass in the club pulses through my heels. The pounding music drowns out everything between us, shakes loose the hurt and feelings until there's no room for anything but this moment. Sweating, wanting, moving, living.

My fingers trace the hard forearm banding around my waist, the lines of ink. "You got a tattoo."

Tyler's face bends close to mine, and my breath hitches as his lips graze my temple. "More than one. You want to see them?"

The crowd presses in on us, and I sense Elle, Rae, Beck, and others. Friends and strangers. Celebration and oblivion.

I want to disappear into it.

"Yes," I whisper.

The hair above the neck of his shirt is damp. Not quite long enough to tug. Some part of me wants to try anyway.

His lips graze my ear, and I tilt my chin back as they drag down my jaw. Heat streaks between my thighs, weaves a rope of need that joins us together, as I move against him in the dark.

He's moving too, holding me, pressing against me.

We're action, reaction. Like musicians who've never played together, attuned to each other because this melody we're weaving depends on it.

There's nothing outside this club. My beautiful

boy, my twisted muse, my rebel prince is gone, but the man holding me is here.

He doesn't give an inch, hands possessive on my hips, holding me against his hardness.

I have a sudden vision of Tyler dragging me into one of these dark corners, yanking up my skirt, and fucking me to the driving rhythm of the bass, our sounds swallowed up by the music around us.

I turn my face more to meet his gaze, and his expression hits me square in the gut.

His lashes are half-lowered, his jaw tight with restraint and hunger, those dangerous eyes filled with emotion I can't read in the dark.

When Tyler speaks again, it's a vibration against my hair.

"Seventy-eight."

I focus on the warmth of his skin through his shirt, the steady echo of his heartbeat. "Seventy-eight what?"

"Seventy-eight times I wrote to you and didn't send them. Once I even drove to Dallas to see you."

My fingers freeze in shock on his neck, and my hips stop swaying under his hands.

*Tyler came to see me?*

Emotions blur together in my chest, my stomach, each one colliding with the next—grief, sadness, love, gratitude.

I blink back the sudden stinging.

He doesn't get to say that as if it can make everything better.

He can't take back that he left. We can't go back to a time when we were innocent and wanting. I'll never again be that earnest girl, and he won't be that guarded boy.

In the DJ booth, I see Rae watching the crowd. At the bar, Elle's talking with Beck, their gazes flicking to us, then away.

Once more, I start to move to the music.

I cover Tyler's hands with my smaller ones, threading my fingers in the spaces between his and squeezing them. I pull one hand off me and bring it to my lips, pressing an open-mouthed kiss to his palm.

I feel his reluctant groan against my back.

I do the same with the other palm, rubbing my ass against him at the same time.

This time, his teeth capture my earlobe, making me shiver. "You're teasing me."

"Then ask me to stop." I turn my profile toward him, rewarded by his hot mouth on my cheek, trailing dangerously close to the corner of my lips.

"No." His breath mingles with mine. "I want you."

I take a moment to feel those words settle into my body. My arousal swells, throbbing like the music around us.

I want him too.

*But that's not what this is about, and wanting was never our problem.*

I turn to face him, pulling out of his hold.

His tortured expression is full of desire and something more meaningful. It's that something that calls to me, that has me second-guessing my plan.

I ignore it and lift my chin, my heart still hammering in my chest as I take a steadying breath. "Good. Now you know what it feels like."

It takes every bit of self-control in me to turn and walk away without looking back.

# 8

# Annie

I knew going home for the weekend would be a minefield, but it's even more treacherous than I imagined. All my dad's friends are in one house to celebrate his award, and the table is full of friends bursting with well-intentioned and dangerous curiosity.

"How're classes?" Nina, my dad's former tour manager, asks me over dinner Saturday night.

"Hard, but at least they're interesting," I say. "I have two essays and a project due before midterms." *So far, so good.* I take a congratulatory bite of fettucine, cooked to perfection by the chef Dad and Haley hired when Sophie hit two and Haley started working again full-time.

"How's Pen?" Haley asks.

My stomach untwists a little. "Already planning her platform for student government. And shopping like crazy."

"You're rooming with your friend?" Nina asks, and I take a slow breath.

"Er... no. My roommate's kind of different," I tell them. "I think she sees me as competition."

Uncle Ryan cocks his head. "Didn't figure an undergraduate degree was so ruthless."

Every pair of eyes turns to me, including my dad's from the head of the table.

"Everything's a competition, Uncle Ry." I drain my water glass before reaching for the bottle of bourbon at the center of the table.

My dad narrows his eyes as I pour into the empty glass.

"Enough," he says when there's half an inch inside.

I roll my eyes. "I'm an adult."

"You're still my kid."

The conversation turns to the lifetime achievement award my dad won, and I'm both relieved the pressure is off and fascinated by the discussion.

Across the table, Sophie plays with her pink plastic spoon, her dark hair in pigtails and her eyes bright with enthusiasm for everything. Her bow mouth lifts in an incandescent smile, and I can't resist grinning back.

It sounds trite, but she's seriously growing up so fast. She walks and babbles and tries to make sense of the world around her.

*Good luck with that, Soph.*

I decided on the plane home I'd use this weekend to warm Dad up to the idea of Vanier, but I haven't decided how that will work.

After dinner, I catch Dad in his office talking with Ryan. I creep up to the half-open door to hear them speaking in hushed tones.

"What's going on?" I ask.

Ryan clears his throat. "Nothing. Good to see you, kid." He drops a kiss on top of my head like I'm still ten years old before heading out the door.

"Well?" I ask again once Ryan's gone, squaring my shoulders.

"It's shop talk." Dad goes to the fireplace, kneels before it, and stacks logs inside.

*Now's my chance to talk to him.*

I drop to my knees at his side. "You can talk business in front of me. If I'm old enough to drink at home, I'm old enough for that."

He adjusts the logs, adding kindling from the

bin nearby. "It's about our catalogue. Wicked has the rights to some of our early tracks and is planning to record them with new artists. I'm trying to go through lawyers to get them back, but so far nothing."

I grab a newspaper from the stack and wad up a sheet, encouraged by his admission. "So, write new songs."

He shakes his head as he tucks the sheets I pass him around the edges of the kindling. "It's not that easy, Annie. I've been out of the business a long time."

He rises to get a match from the box on the mantel and lights the edges of the paper in the fireplace. The flames lick at them, trying to find their way.

I rise too. On a surge of bravado, I reach into my pocket and pull out a sheet of paper I was scribbling on the plane. "I want you to look at something."

"What is this?"

I shift on my feet. "A poem. Or a song."

He reads it again while I hold my breath.

I've imagined this moment so many times. I've imagined his response—surprise, admiration, pride.

"You spend all day reading and writing essays for school, and when you're done you want to do this?"

Hurt lodges in my throat. "It doesn't have to be a hobby. I could do this for real. Like you did."

He folds his arms. "Annie, I went into the industry because an offer came and I was too young and desperate to turn it down." He retrieves his bourbon from the desk. "You've seen the brightness of the music industry but never the dark. If you had any idea how many threats, how many lawsuits, how many people wanted to use me... I'm grateful my career brought me my family, my friends, the ability to make something that affects people—it's not a question of that. But that kind of life has a cost, and I would never want that for you."

"Given how you grew up, I would've thought you'd want me to have the choice you didn't. And I do have that choice."

His gaze narrows. "I don't want you to pay it without understanding what you're signing up for."

Frustration flows through me. "But don't you think I pay it anyway being your kid? I never got to choose that part."

The words hang between us until he holds the paper out for me. "Tell Haley and the others I'll be out in a few minutes. I need to return a call."

I take the sheet from him, then he grabs me in a quick one-armed hug before turning back to his desk.

*He doesn't get it. He doesn't see how it could be.*

*And tonight, there's nothing I can do to change his mind.*

I ball up the sheet of lyrics and toss it into the fire before heading for the door.

---

"I know you spent the entire weekend lying to your family," Elle whispers as we take our seats in our entertainment class Monday.

The pen I'm retrieving from my bag falls from my fingers and rolls toward her desk. "What?"

She picks it up, cocking her head. "You pretended to be present when you were really mentally jerking off to Tyler Adams."

Warmth floods me as I take the pen back.

"You did have some hot chemistry before you walked away from him Friday morning," she presses. "Stone cold."

*"Seventy-eight times I wrote to you."*

In my mind, Tyler Adams had walked away and never looked back. If that wasn't true...

I keep telling myself that changes nothing, but it means he cared. Even when he was going through whatever he was going through, he thought of me.

When I walked away, I didn't mean to be petty, but I wanted him to feel a tiny, momentary slice of the hell he'd put me through.

"Whatever your plan was," Elle continues, "the guy looked seriously bummed you were gone. He didn't dance with another girl all night."

Her words leave my body tingling. Tyler still brings up a ton of emotions in me, and it's not only about who he was. Judging from what I heard at Leo's last week, he's even more talented than he was a year ago. He's more confident too, more grown up.

We both are.

But just because he had a harder time leaving me than I thought doesn't change anything for us now.

It can't.

My gaze pulls to the door when Rae enters,

scanning for a seat. The only remaining one is next to us, and she drops into it.

The instructor starts her lecture, and I try to tune into the discussion in class about how to set yourself apart while building a brand.

"So, this family weekend," Elle says to me at the end of class. "It was big?"

"Ten people, plus my dad and stepmom and little sister. Food and booze and sugar comas." I tuck my notebook away in my bag.

"My weekend was here, watching movies and living on noodles. Your life sounds like heaven."

The image of my dad reading my words and handing them back to me floods my mind—him tossing them into the fire, watching them dissolve.

"Not even close." I shoulder my bag and start for the door.

"I know you have issues with your dad," Elle says, "but if he's breathing? He shows up? Sounds like an epic father figure."

Before I can respond, she takes off down the hall, leaving me with my mouth hanging open.

Rae's appearance at my side makes me jump. "You going to her set tomorrow? She's got twenty minutes at Comedy Palace."

I shake my head in surprise. I'd figured Elle would've told me about something like that.

Rae starts to take off, but I grab her bag first.

"Hey," I say on impulse as she turns, raising a brow. "I know I'm not your favorite person. I know all you want is for me to be gone so you can have a single room. And your voodoo might even work—"

Her black-rimmed eyes round. "My what?"

*Shit*. "The dolls. On your headboard."

"You think they're voodoo dolls?" Her face slackens in disbelief. "They're for Etsy. I sell them."

"Oh. Fuck. I'm sorry." I flush with embarrassment. "Anyway, maybe we could go to this show together. To support Elle."

Rae flips me off, and my stomach sinks.

Three paces away, she turns to call over her shoulder, "You know where I live. You can pick me up at eight."

I follow Rae up the stairs from the subway later that night. "You got into the DJ booth at the club on Friday night. How'd you even do that?"

We fall into step together on the sidewalk. "Trade secrets," she says, but her voice turns wistful. "I'm gonna set the world on fire. You're not making music, you're making a vibe. It's all about mood and energy and tempo. Your tracks have an energy; your people have an energy. They're like atoms. Every combination of people has its own sense, its own chaos. It's all about finding those three people."

"Three people?" I'm intrigued. Those are the most words I've heard my roommate string together in my presence, and now that she's talking, I don't want her to stop.

"Three people who set the tone for everyone else. You can always find three people in a crowd. No one will admit they're watching them or even knows consciously. But they are. If you're spinning, you gotta get to know them. Live inside them. You move them, they move the room."

Before I can ask more, we're outside the doors of the venue.

Comedy Palace is smaller than Leo's, and Rae scans the foyer as if she's looking for her three people even now.

We find a table at the back. We're barely seated when two hands land on my shoulders and I whirl in my seat.

Beck grins down at me. "Hey, ladies."

"What are you doing here?" I ask, feeling the smile pull across my face already.

"We were invited."

Before I can ask who "we" is, my gaze lands on the guy next to him, and I stiffen.

Tyler's dressed in jeans and a dark-blue button-down that makes his chocolate eyes look even darker.

But the most surprising part isn't his presence —it's how not disappointed I am to see him.

"Don't take this the wrong way, but by who?" I ask lightly.

Tyler looks between me and Rae, who picks at her leather jacket innocently.

*Every combination of people has its own sense, its own chaos.*

Apparently, Rae liked our brand of chaos enough to recreate it.

The guys grab chairs and pull them up to our table. Tyler's forced to tuck his in close to mine so Rae can still get out and head for the bar.

"You want?" she asks Beck, jerking her head.

"Yeah, sure." He follows her.

"Did you tell Jax and Haley you're at Vanier?" Tyler asks me when Rae's gone.

His bluntness has me straightening. "No."

"You're going to have to."

"Why do you care?"

"Because I care about you." Something flickers behind Tyler's eyes. "And I care about them," he goes on.

Before I can argue, Rae and Beck return, and the house lights dim. The first performer is a guy who talks about his pets for the entire time.

Elle's the second performer. We cheer as she takes the stage.

"Here's the thing about being twenty in New York—everyone assumes you came from some piece-of-shit city to be an overpaid trader or an underpaid actor. I take offense to that. I came from the country to be an unpaid comedian."

The audience chuckles as she strolls across the stage, the lights following her.

"I have three younger brothers, but my dad died when I was ten."

My stomach falls, but she continues.

"So, I had to keep my mom laughing. Because them wetting the bed every night wasn't doing it."

The backs of my eyes burn as I think of our exchange in the hallway earlier about my dad, how I gave her shit for making him sound better than he is.

I'd asked her about her baggage once, and she said it was too much to talk about.

I duck my face to swipe at my damp eyes, and my gaze finds Tyler's, holds it.

He's feeling what I am—compassion, sadness, understanding, and I'm glad he's here.

I force myself to focus on the rest of Elle's set, then the remaining performers, and the heaviness gives way to laughter.

Everyone has their own pain. Elle uses it to connect people, weaves the hard times in with the good ones.

When the houselights come up, I pull out my phone to text Elle, but Rae grabs my arm. "Don't. This wasn't about us."

The crowd outside is laughing and tipsy as we wind our way out to the street. I fall into step next to Beck, behind Tyler and Rae.

"Let's get something to eat," Beck decides.

We find a diner a block away. I hold the door for Rae, and she shakes her head, holding up a pack of cigarettes from her jacket pocket.

Before the three of us can find a booth, Beck's phone rings.

He checks the screen and starts toward the door. "Order me a Coke," he calls. "I'll be back."

Tyler and I slide into the booth across from one another.

There are people of every kind in the restaurant. There's an elderly couple across from a young couple, and I wonder what they're talking about, what their lives are like, if they act brave in the daylight, if questions they can't answer start to circle their minds when the lights go out.

"I know I have to tell him," I blurt, turning back to find Tyler watching me, impassive. "But I want him to understand why I'm doing it. I want him to see that I'm good enough to make a career at this. Last year, I was so focused on getting into Vanier. It was this singular thing I could picture. I told myself everything would be easy once I was surrounded by people who got what it meant to want this life, to be on the stage. But now that I'm here, it's not easy. Maybe it never will be again. Do you ever feel that way?"

My voice is just audible over the chatter and clinking cutlery and plates. I sink my shoulders back against the booth.

I feel more vulnerable than when he found my Polaroids, than when I stood in front of him naked, because this it the truth—the thing that haunts me, that I don't have an answer to. It's not my past, it's my future.

"More than you know." Tyler shifts forward in his seat. His shoulders are tight under his button-down. "When I left Dallas for New York, I had a contract with a label. Was supposed to start in the studio a week in. But my third day here, I got a call from Philly. My dad wrecked his car driving drunk and was in a coma in the hospital."

My body goes cold, but he continues before I can process. "I went back to Philly. Stared at his face for two days, couldn't decide whether I wanted to save him or pull the plug—because the prick listed me to make those decisions, after all we've been through. In the end, I told them to do everything they could. For a week, they did. He died anyway."

My gut twists tighter, until all my organs are one giant knot of sadness and rage—sadness for Tyler and what he must have felt, rage for knowing he went through it alone.

"I took care of arrangements. Got a loan to cover the funeral." He grimaces, shoving a hand through his dark hair. "I figured I'd pay the medical bills off with money from my contract. But by the time I got back to New York, I'd been gone two weeks. Zeke was calling, I wasn't answering, and when I showed up at his door, he was pissed."

"He must've understood when you told him," I murmur.

"I didn't tell him. It was my problem, my shame, my decision." His voice fills with grief, and every part of me wants to reach across the table and hold him even though I know I can't.

"There was only one person I wanted to see." He shifts back in his seat, exhaling hard, and those beautiful eyes deepen with an emotion that has my heart kicking in my chest. "It was the middle of July. I'd been keeping my distance from you, telling myself you'd be better off and to give you space. But I couldn't do it anymore. I needed to know you were okay, that something I cared about was right in the world. When I got to Dallas, I saw you outside the library with some guy"—the disbelief in his voice has me aching all over again—"looking like you didn't have a care in the world."

I swallow, trying to process even a tenth of what he's giving me and failing. My fingers trace the placemat in front of me, across the bottom, up the sides. "He worked with me," I offer at last.

"He made you smile. And that was what I

wanted for you. I didn't want to intrude, to make you suffer more than you already had. So, I left."

My throat closes up. Of all the reasons I'd considered why Tyler hadn't called, that wasn't one of them.

I'd been feeling like shit that entire summer, was devastated to feel alone—truly alone—for the first time in a long time.

But now I understand how hard this was for him, too.

Tyler's hands fold in front of him on the table, but they're tense.

"Zeke terminated my contract. Told me to figure my shit out. I had a contact at Vanier and was able to get in last minute. So, I figured I'd take classes until Zeke changed his mind.

"The thing is, when I was here, I wasn't really here. My music had lost something. That's the problem when you start depending on other people. Like my dad blamed me for interfering with his music by existing."

I trace the top line of the placemat with my finger, and when I get to the center, a few inches of cheap countertop is all that keeps our hands from brushing.

I swallow the urge to bridge that distance when he continues.

"There's a difference between caring for people and ignoring your responsibilities," I say. "Working with people, relying on them... it's a beautiful thing." I cut a look over my shoulder toward the door. "Like you and Beck. He's so loyal to you, and I can see you've earned it."

His heavy gaze meets mine, and the lump in my throat expands until I can't breathe.

"I need you to know something. That day you saw me in Dallas," I go on, "I might've been smiling, but it hurt. Every smile for months was like swallowing glass. I understand why you left, but if you think for a second it didn't tear me up, you were wrong. I wish you'd said goodbye."

Tyler tugs on his hair, eyes squeezing shut. "Nah. See, if I'd said goodbye, I wouldn't have gone."

This time, I can't stop myself from reaching for his hand. His skin is warm under mine, and his chocolate gaze finds me.

I'm living for the feel of his skin on mine.

"When I saw you walk past that rehearsal room at Vanier last spring," he says roughly, "I thought I was hallucinating." Tyler's hand tightens on mine, his lips twitching with self-mocking. "I thought I wished you here. And you can hate me all you want, but I'm glad you came."

His words slam into me. "What about the girl you were with?"

"She was a friend. We were more for a little while, but…" Tyler shakes his head. "She wasn't you. No one's ever been you."

I'm drowning in emotions, and I can't pick one out from the rest or figure out what this means going forward.

The one thing I know is that the story I told myself about how we were, how we ended, was wrong. Our past isn't the story I told myself.

*Maybe our future isn't either.*

Tyler's eyes warm on mine, and I wonder if he's thinking the same thing.

Beck drops into the booth, and I pull back my hand.

"Got an audition," he chirps.

I glance toward the front door to see Elle and Rae walk inside. Elle looks startled when she sees all of us.

"You were great tonight," I tell her when she pulls up next to the table.

Her lips curve, embarrassed. "Thanks. I didn't know you guys were going to be there."

"What can I get you?" the waitress asks when I shift over to let my roommate and friend in. The waitress goes around to Elle and Rae and Beck before coming to me.

I turn the question over for a long moment before answering. "How're your cheese fries?"

"They're great," she answers with a smile.

"I'll take a small."

"Make it a large," Tyler says smoothly, and I sneak a look at him under my lashes.

His expression is filled with an intensity that steals my breath, but for the first time this year, it doesn't leave me feeling tortured.

It leaves me hopeful.

The waitress leaves, and my friends start to talk about one of the other performers from tonight's show.

I train my attention on Elle's animated face, but I'm only half listening when something brushes my leg.

*Tyler.*

His calf against my knee.

It was probably an accident. Even with the five of us in this booth, it's not crowded.

Except he's not moving. The single innocent touch has my entire body heating.

All it would take would be a tiny shift on my part to break that connection.

Instead, I stretch out my other leg and link my feet around his ankle so neither of us can move away.

9

———

# *Tyler*

"**W**here you going this early? Breakfast at Vanier?" Beck's voice comes from the kitchen Thursday morning.

"Nah, I can make use of the now-functioning fridge," I reply. "There's some non-moldy cream cheese in there."

I pack my guitar in its case and give myself a quick once-over in the bedroom mirror on the badly painted dresser that came with the apartment. My shirt is not only clean but ironed, and my hair's doing more or less what I want.

I'll take it as a win.

"Yeah, but there's nothing to put it on. Except

an overripe banana." Beck peers inside as I pass him, guitar in tow.

"Figured you'd be into that," I say as I head for the front door.

"Overripe is a problem," Beck says. "I prefer them young. Firm."

"And I will never ask again." I drop my guitar case and set my phone on the counter to grab my jacket.

The fridge has been fixed since Monday, but we haven't gotten anything resembling groceries.

We've been busy.

Beck landed a string of auditions and even won a commercial. I've started working on my show-case audition in earnest. I have a song in mind, but I'm not satisfied it's what I need to land the closing spot and score the visibility and ten grand that would put a dent in my dad's hospital bills.

My phone buzzes, and Beck grabs it before I can. "Tyler: 'Got a line on a rehearsal room at 8 a.m.'"

I shrug into the coat, his gaze cutting back to me. "Wait," he says, "You not only scored a rehearsal room but you're willing to share it with someone?"

I reach for my shoes. "It's not a big deal."

"Annie: 'Long as it won't cramp your style to practice with the competition.'" Beck hollers. "Oh, you're trying to move in on my girl."

One shoe on, I snatch the phone back. "I told you, she's not your girl."

"You're so far into her it's a wonder you can speak. Because your lips are glued to her ass," Beck explains at my blank stare as I tuck the phone away and put on the other shoe. "Or other places."

A week ago, Beck would've been right. I was fighting the attraction. Her dancing with me on Beck's birthday—even if she did it to prove a point—meant I couldn't fall asleep all weekend without jerking off to the thought of her.

But the night at Comedy Palace changed things.

*"I understand why you left, but if you think for a second it didn't tear me up, you were wrong."*

The way she looked at me, the way our hands brushed when we walked side by side on the way home, gave me something I haven't felt in a long time.

*Hope.*

Since vowing to win back my contract, I've been running on determination, conviction, even a need for vindication.

I didn't realize how dark those feelings were until I had something bright to compare them to.

"We've been texting all week," I tell him. "And we've had lunch twice at Vanier."

"Sounds serious." He flutters his eyelashes.

"She's the first girl I ever fell for."

I reach for my bag, but Beck's groan has me look up.

"Slow your roll," he says. "I knew you knew her before this year. A high school girlfriend from Philly?"

"No." I exhale hard. "She's Jax Jamieson's kid."

His jaw hits the floor. "Well, fuck me. She's the one who messed you up before you came here. I get it. She's pretty fucking great." His response has the hairs on my neck lifting. "But I'm not gonna go there, because you guys have some major unresolved shit."

"It's past tense."

"Really? Because I saw how you looked at her the other night," Beck says. "That wasn't a 'past tense' kind of look. That was a 'present perfect' kind of look."

"You don't know what that means."

"Sure, I do. You'd like to *have been getting some* for the last two weeks."

I shake my head as I start out the door. "Just eat the banana, Beck. I'll catch you tonight."

Our neighborhood's not the safest, but in daylight it's fine. I don't notice any of it this morning on my way to Vanier. Instead, I'm thinking of Annie.

Beck's right. The past tense feelings are blurring with the present tense ones. The more I talk to her, the harder it gets to convince myself there's nothing between us.

But just because I'm attracted to her doesn't mean I'd jump into a relationship with her or that she would with me.

I have to think twice before letting someone in again. I fucked up my career when I moved to New York last fall and spun out, and while some of it was about what happened with my dad? A lot of it was about her.

I can't afford to set myself up for that again.

I head to school, and an hour later, I'm in the rehearsal room running my audition song when a knock comes. I get up from my stool, guitar in one hand, and open the door.

My breath sticks in my throat.

Annie's dark hair is piled up on her head, a few pieces loose from the bun I want to tug out just to see it fall in waves around her shoulders. Her cheeks are flushed. She's wearing leggings and a denim shirt with the top two buttons undone, and the way her backpack straps tug on the fabric reveals a tantalizing glimpse of the curve of her breasts. A chain disappears beneath the clothes.

I want to follow it with my tongue.

"There's a price to enter," I say, my voice remarkably level.

She angles her chin up. "I'm not going to blow you."

All the blood in my body goes south.

I take back every thought about wanting to rewind time, to get back the girl I knew a year ago.

I want *this* Annie Jamieson, the one with dancing eyes who says she's not going to blow me as if she's actually considered letting me stick my cock between those beautiful lips.

As if the right circumstances might make her consider it again.

Oblivious to my thoughts, she holds out one of two coffees. "My final offer."

I take one with my free hand and let her in.

She crosses the room, dropping onto the piano bench. "I thought we could pause the competition thing for an hour. I could play my piece, and you could play yours. You know, give each other notes."

I shift onto the stool. The rooms aren't big, so I'm only a few steps away from her and the piano.

"Deal," I say. "You start."

She turns to the piano and begins. The melody is pretty, but her voice grabs me and won't let go.

I'm glad she's facing away because I don't need her to see what her art does to me.

And it is art, what she creates. Every note and inflection, every breath, all of it spills between us, shapes something new and magical I couldn't resist if I wanted to.

"Those words," I say when she's done. "I recognize some of them from the pictures in your room."

Annie shifts on the bench. "I decided I might as well use them for something."

"It's a good song."

"But it's not right." She grabs her lower lip in her teeth. "Let me hear yours."

I hesitate only a moment before picking out a song on my guitar.

It's not the one I've been rehearsing, but something new.

Annie leans closer, listening. "I like it."

Riding a wave of impulsiveness, I add my voice overtop.

*Her words.* The ones she just sang, but the music's different.

She doesn't say anything for a verse, then another.

Finally, I stop playing and meet her gaze, my heart hammering in my chest.

Her lips are parted, her expression coloring in awe. "What did you do?"

"I changed it a little."

I half expect her to freak on me, like the guys at the studio do when I mess with their work.

Instead, Annie grabs a pen from her bag and drags the piano bench over to my stool, close enough our thighs touch.

If she feels me tighten next to her, she doesn't acknowledge it. My sleeves are rolled up, and she takes my arm, holding my hand, and starts to write.

"I have more words since I took those pictures," she explains as she works. "Better ones."

Her skin's warm on mine as she fills my bare forearm with ink, wrist to elbow. I don't stop her.

Each phrase has my heart thudding dully in my chest, has me looking between her bent head and my skin, has me longing for something I don't understand and don't need to.

"There." She shifts back onto the bench.

I want to reach for her, but instead I reach for my guitar.

Then I play.

The words are music, flowing from my fingers like water.

My thigh's still touching hers, our bodies inches apart, as she joins in singing at the chorus.

Her attention is on me, not the guitar. I can feel her gaze—I've always felt her gaze.

It's like the sun on a summer day.

I thrill to it, thrive on it.

When we finish, we both exhale hard.

"Tyler," she murmurs. "That was..."

*Spectacular. Raw. Fucking incredible.*

I can't voice the words because they're too big and too small for what I'm feeling.

She straightens in her seat, pressing her lips together. Her face is tight, but her eyes are bright, expressive. "I can't perform that. It's your music."

"Sure you can."

Annie seems to wrestle with it. "If I land the closing spot, I'll give you the money. You said you have bills from your dad. That would help."

"No. It would be yours." Still, the fact that she's thinking of me makes my gut twist.

There it is. The reason I can't ignore her.

She makes me feel that I'm more than I am, like I matter just for being here.

"What about your song?" Annie prompts.

"It needs work."

"I can help."

"No." She looks hurt, so I explain. "Being here with you like this… it feels like old times."

"You say that like it's a bad thing. We had some good times," she murmurs.

They weren't bad at all, and that's the problem.

I can't say that it reminds me of the easy intimacy we used to have—letting each other in, working together, relying on one another.

*Craving each other.*

My attention drops to her necklace. Despite the voice in my head insisting this is a terrible idea, I hook a finger around the chain, drawing it out of her shirt. Her breath catches as it drags up her skin, revealing the glass pendant.

The troubling familiarity shifts into recognition, a key sliding into a lock as I turn the pendant in my fingers. "Your dad's roses."

"The day after I got grounded, we hung out by

the pool, and you carried me up the driveway, and you gave me that rose."

Surprise slams into me—that she remembers it, that she kept it, that she wears it.

"You were a jerk that day," Annie goes on, oblivious to the emotions roiling inside me.

When I reply, my voice is an octave lower. "I was a jerk because I wanted you so much. Wanting you makes me grumpy."

She arches a brow, her full lips twitching. "Then I guess it's a good thing we never slept together."

My next breath is ragged. "I said wanting you made me a jerk. If I'd had you, I would've been…"

I trail off, but her half-lidded gaze roams my face before falling to my mouth.

"What?" she murmurs.

*Whole.*

The word fills my mind without permission.

"I think you would've been happy," she finishes.

The truth of her words echoes through my chest. It's impossible to rewind to a time before this girl knew me.

If we were dust in the air, her soul would call to mine.

I drop the necklace, reaching up to play with a strand of hair that's escaped her bun. "I used to wonder if you went to prom. How you would've worn your hair if you did."

"I wore it up."

My chest tightens. "Did you go alone?"

"No."

I wrap the strand around my finger, tugging. "Did you dance with him?"

Her eyes darken. "Yeah."

"Kiss him?"

Annie nods slowly, and I know she's not thinking of her prom—at least, not only.

She's remembering the night I took Carly to prom when she asked me the same thing.

I inch closer until we're nearly touching so she's forced to tilt her face up to hold my gaze.

The next question isn't mine to ask, but neither were the two before it.

"Did you fuck him?"

Those expressive amber eyes color with something I can't name.

The answer's there on her face, and I hate it. I hate knowing I could've been her first and wasn't. I have no right to expect she would have saved herself for me, but the thought of her with another guy drives me crazy.

"Tyler—"

"I wanted to give you that night. So many times in my head, I did."

Her lips part, and I want to devour them. Her unsteady inhale makes my cock twitch.

We thought life was so complicated a year ago. Nothing was complicated.

But no matter what I resolved when I walked away from her on that sunny day in Dallas, I won't pretend she didn't leave her mark on me.

"You better play me your song," she says at last, her voice rough at the edges, "or we're going to run out of time."

I unwind the hair and tuck it behind her ear.

Then I reach for my guitar.

# 10

# Annie

"You going to 'practice' with Tyler again?"

I'm walking past Elle's open dorm door with my bag and jacket when her voice has me pulling up.

I step into her doorway, taking in the sight of my friend reclined on her bed, notebook in her lap. "What's with the finger quotes?" I ask.

"You've been spending every second together all week. If your strategy is to get close enough to backstab the competition, you're running out of time."

"We're competing, but our biggest competition is the dozens of other people auditioning."

She cocks her head. "You realize there's only one closing spot."

Which is why even though we've practiced together a few times, those long looks and teasing touches have been as far as it's gone.

*"I wanted to give you that night. So many times in my head, I did."*

The recipe for a sleepless night starts with Tyler Adams telling you he thinks about all the things you never did together. I've spent a few hours wrapped in sweaty sheets thinking of them, too.

But I'm thinking about why I'm here at Vanier and my goals. With the auditions happening Monday, the closing spot is close enough I can taste it.

My phone jumps in my pocket with a text.

**Unknown: It's Finn. Meet me out front of the school in fifteen minutes for intensive.**

**Annie: I thought we were meeting tomorrow?**

**Unknown: Change of plans. If you can do right now, it'll be worth your while.**

I tell Elle about the message. "Is this normal for faculty to take students off campus for weird evening sessions?" she asks.

"I'm not sure Finn follows the rules." But I'm intrigued.

"We're all still going out tomorrow night, right?" Elle asks as I start toward the hall.

"Yeah. My friend Pen and the guy she's seeing suggested a place they like."

I go down to the first floor and turn toward the main lobby. A black car's pulled up at the curb, and the window buzzes down, revealing Finn inside the backseat. I shift into the car, pull the door behind me.

"Some people think being double-booked is a conflict," he says once I'm in. "I think it's an opportunity. I'm playing a show tonight. Figured you could keep me company."

I glance out the window as the city passes us by. "I haven't been to a show in... months."

"Then you're in for a treat."

Two hours later, we're at a venue in Jersey. The audience is a few thousand people—loud, screaming. They're not here for me, but from the moment I take up a post in the shadows backstage, I close my eyes and pretend they are.

*This is what it feels like to make a name for yourself.*

Finn runs off partway through, sweating, and checks the set list while he gets touch-ups. "I know what you're thinking."

"What's that?"

"That the purpose of your intensive at Vanier is to hone your craft, not mine."

"Well, yeah, but this is fun," I admit.

With a grin, he points at the next track on the set list. "You know this track?"

I nod.

"Drop in on it." There's a cocky angle to his grin, and I blink at him in astonishment.

"I'm not warmed up, I'm in the wrong clothes, and I don't have performance makeup."

But he jerks his head as he jogs back on stage, and I slowly follow him. His bassist steps back, gesturing to the mic. So, I take it.

I've been on stage a dozen times in the last few years, but none of the small productions I've done have felt like this. This is freedom—an orgy of lights and sound and love and feeling.

It's not my song, but the audience sings along, pulsing right there with me.

Backstage after, Finn downs a bottle of water.

"That was incredible," I gush.

"This is the contemporary music program. Not 'break your back bending over your violin for twenty years until someone lets you play second in a symphony.' You saw that crowd. You think they'd pay two hundred bucks a seat to see Mozart?"

"Mozart's dead."

"Exactly." He grins.

"Listen," I start. "I want to run my audition piece for the showcase by you once more. I've been making some changes, and I'd love your input. Would you have time tomorrow?"

Finn cocks his head. "You didn't hear."

"Hear what?" My heart kicks in my chest.

"First years are being disqualified from auditioning this year. " He reaches for his phone, swipes through a few screens. "Looks like it was just in a faculty email that went around today. The first years who signed up will be contacted tomorrow."

"But... why?"

"One of the professors adjudicating landed a last minute gig and can't sit for the full number of auditions. The dean decided to focus on second years, since that's who the showcase is for anyway." He shrugs.

Disbelief has my throat swelling, my chest tightening. This was my chance, the perfect opportunity to prove why I'm here and get noticed for my own talent, not my name.

"That's bullshit," I blurt. "Some of us need this chance."

"I'm with you." Finn holds the door for me, and I force myself to walk through. "Oh, one more thing— I'm gonna be gone the week after the showcase in November. Playing three gigs in LA and San Francisco. I could get you tickets if you're interested."

I try to focus on his words, but I can't bring myself to care, because my dreams are going up in smoke.

***

"This is where you hang out?" Rae cranes her neck from her spot in the booth to peer around the packed bar the next night.

Pen nods. "It's mostly Columbia students."

"There's no stage," Elle notes.

Rae, Pen, Elle, and I are crowded around a booth Saturday night. I'm trying to enjoy the atmosphere, but it's hard given I'm still reeling from the fact that all my work this semester—hell, for the last two years—will come to nothing.

I need this showcase to remind myself I made the right choice. That I'm at Vanier for a reason and that I have a chance of making it in this business on my own merit.

I glance toward the bar, catching a glimpse of the guy Pen's seeing with Tyler, Beck, and a couple of guys from school. "Dave seems cool," I say, forcing myself to think of my friends.

"He is. I never thought I'd date an engineer. I always figured they'd be too…"

"Cocky?"

"Reductionist."

The guys at the bar are all objectively good-looking. Pen's guy is cute and preppy, Beck's got that "I'm hot and I know how to use it" look, but Tyler's the most commanding, his Henley pulling tight over his shoulders and chest. He's still the rebel prince, but he's opened up. Whether he knows it or not, he's let this place in, let Beck and the others in.

Some girls interrupt the guys, talking and flirting, and my hand clenches around my glass.

"Oh, I wondered how long this would take," Pen drawls.

Elle leans in. "What?"

I stare at my high school friend pointedly, but she waves me off.

"Tyler and Annie go back."

Rae narrows her eyes, and Elle scoffs, "This is new information."

"Yes, *Penelope*," I warn.

Pen holds up a hand. "Don't try to scare me with your four syllables. I'm not talking out of turn here. Just saying you guys have some especially angsty baggage."

My attention drags back to the girl smiling at Tyler.

"She's thinking about dragging that girl across the floor by her hair," Rae deadpans. Elle laughs, and Pen grins.

I have no right to feel that way, but as we've rehearsed together over the past week, it's gotten harder and harder not to feel something for him.

"What's he like in bed?" Elle asks, and I choke on my drink.

"We never slept together," I say when I stop coughing.

"Oh, that does explain the tension." Elle cocks her head as I squirm in my seat, tugging the hem of my skirt that's riding high up my legs.

"I bet he'd learn everything you like, memorize it, use it all against you to get his way."

Rae's words have me flushing, averting my gaze.

Forgive me for not bringing a change of underwear to this venue.

My gaze drags from the girl and over to Tyler, his strong shoulders, handsome profile.

He's beyond sexy. Thinking about him is sexy. Talking about him is sexy.

Breathing the same air in the same room is sexy.

The guy in question turns his head and catches me staring. His gaze skims down and back up, as if he can see me press my thighs together under the table.

I can't look away.

If I'm honest, I still have feelings for Tyler.

But even if I think there's a chance he feels the same way, that's not why we're here. We have our dreams, and we've both given up things to pursue them.

The waitress comes by to see if we want more drinks. "You guys are Vanier students. I was one. Acting."

"Do you work?" Rae says.

"Mostly, I'm here. I get good hours." She winks, but her smile seems forced.

We order another round, and she disappears.

*That's the reality*, I remind myself. *It's easy to want this life. It's harder to make it happen. Especially when your plan for getting it done—the showcase— gets yanked out from under you.*

Before I've taken another sip of my drink, hands settle on my neck. I jump as something soft brushes my ear.

"You've been quiet tonight." Tyler's not in my line of sight, but I feel his touch on my bare skin, smell his familiar cedar scent.

Before I can respond, he lifts me out of the booth and sets me by his side.

"Tell me what's up."

"What's up is you win. Congratulations." I pull my phone from my bag and hold out the email I got from the dean's office today.

I shove a hand through my hair, looking past him while he reads it. "They're not letting me audition," I say under my breath. "New policy."

"This isn't happening." The edge in his voice does nothing to soothe my frustration.

I take the phone back and tuck it away. "Whatever. It was a long shot anyway."

I try to brush past him, but he cages me in with his arms. "Tyler… there's nothing we can do."

"Audition with me."

My mind goes blank as I take in his angry face. "Wait, what?"

"We can do your song together."

"They won't let us—"

"Then we'll make them."

"But what if they disqualify you?"

He narrows his gaze. "Let them try."

My chest expands with emotions I can't name. "You want to change your audition with three days left to rehearse."

"Yeah. I do."

I study him, trying to figure out where Tyler went and who this reckless man in his place is.

But all I see is the same guy I've always known, with a flash of rebelliousness in his dark gaze that has a shimmer of hope starting low in my stomach.

I throw my arms around his neck, inhaling his familiar scent and trying not to be distracted by the heat and hardness of his body. My eyes burn. "Thank you."

His arms wrap around me, too, and my heart feels lighter than it has in two days.

"We can rehearse all day tomorrow. We can use

the apartment. Beck will understand."

"I promise I'll do you proud."

"I know you will."

Over his shoulder, I notice a pool table at the other end of the bar. "But since we're not rehearsing until tomorrow... look what I found."

He turns to look, and his chuckle warms me. "You wanna play pool, Six?"

"With you? Always. I'm gonna kick your ass."

"We'll see about that."

"I can't believe you got that email today and didn't tell me," he chides, following me to the table.

"I didn't want to bring you down or distract you from your own rehearsing. I actually found out yesterday when I went to Finn's show."

He takes two cues off the wall and passes me one. But when he responds, he's guarded. "What part of that's in the curriculum?"

My jaw goes slack with incredulity as I twist the chalk over the end of my cue. "Come on, Tyler. It was a trip. Have you ever heard him? There's a reason Finn Harvey has a gold album."

I brush past him to rack up the balls. I'm bent over, lining up my break when his hand settles between my shoulder blades. "We need stakes."

I shiver, turning to feel his lips brush my ear. "You sound like you've got something in mind."

"I win, you kiss me like you mean it."

I twist so his arms are around me. Tyler tucks a piece of hair behind my ear, sending a jolt of electricity humming through me while his gaze roams my face.

The man who offered to share the spotlight with me. *For* me. No questions asked.

I make a decision there's no going back from.

"Fine. But if I win... you kiss me like you would've if you hadn't walked away that day outside the library in Dallas."

His hand stills, heat flaring behind his eyes.

He gets what this means, that it's an admission I want him, that I want to play out whatever's between us—that I'm every bit as frustrated from the tension that's been building all week, all year.

"Deal."

At a glance, it could seem as if the stakes have vanished, but they're higher than ever.

He wins and I have to show him how much I want him. I'll be the one who's vulnerable, and every part of me that I'd believed had grown up will be tested.

If I win... I get to see what kind of man Tyler

Adams has become since he left me. Because somehow, I know the first touch of his hands, his mouth, will tell me more than the last month has about where he's at.

I want that. So badly.

I take my first shot and sink two. Another three go down as I circle the table before I miss.

"So, tell me about this kiss I'm about to win," Tyler asks as he lines up his first shot.

"It'll have tongue."

Across the table, he lifts his gaze, mouth curving. "I assumed."

I soak in the sight of his powerful body, the simple grace in everything he does. He's masculine and utterly captivating.

"And an ass grab."

Tyler leans over the table. "I didn't ask for an ass grab."

"It's a BOGO kind of deal."

He sinks his target smoothly, and I bite my cheek as he goes on a run of his own.

"You worried?" he muses after sinking the next three.

"Nope."

"You should be."

But eventually, he misses one.

I walk in front of him to find the best angle on the final ball. Once I have it, I toss a look over my shoulder to catch him staring at me.

"I might need help," I say.

His eyes darken, and he closes the distance between us, setting his cue on the edge of the table.

I wait for him to bend over me, his strong body wrapping around me.

*Yes.*

I press my ass against him. My teeth sink into my lip as his scent hits me. I arch my back. "How's my angle?"

His heavy exhale at my ear is pure turn-on. "Shoot already."

The cue slips through my hand...

And I miss.

Now that he has a shot to win it all, the stakes are sinking in.

If he wins, it's going to be more than a single kiss.

Once he touches me again, he'll know how I feel. I won't be able to hold back, and he'll realize I'm torn between wanting him and focusing on my future. I'll be vulnerable in a way I haven't let myself be, not even this past week.

"Annie." Tyler's voice has me turning back to him. "Watch."

My hand squeezes the cue, my palms getting damp as he lines up his shot.

It's harder than the one I had.

*He could miss it.*

He draws back the cue, then slides it through his hand.

Smooth. Sure. Practiced.

My breath catches as I watch the ball roll across the felt, tap the two, and drop it right into the pocket.

Tyler straightens, slow.

My heart flutters in my chest. "I guess you want your kiss."

"No." A hand on my waist has me turning back, catching myself against his chest. Too-knowing chocolate eyes bore into mine. "I want it on our date."

"Our date?" I echo, a step slow.

"Yeah. See, the last time I tried to date you, I fucked it up. We were too young. And I lived in your house. And I don't know if there's a right way to do this, but I want to try."

I search his face, trying to understand the words coming from his lips. "But... dating is a thing people who have time and want to fall in love do. Not people on the edge of finally reaching their dreams after giving up so much to do it."

His gaze sharpens. "You don't think we can have both?"

Of all the things I wondered with Tyler, that he'd want to take me out never occurred to me. It's a beautiful idea, but part of me says it's impossible, that believing that is something the girl who got her heart broken last year would've done, something I'm too smart to do now.

"Tell you what," he says when I don't answer. "We'll have this conversation after our audition."

I nod, swallowing with relief. I take his cue and hang it up with mine. "We should get back to our friends."

"Wait." He catches my wrist before I can pass him. "I changed my mind about that kiss."

His voice is low, a sensual promise as he tugs me against him.

"You want it here?" I look around us.

He backs me against the pool table until my ass rests on the edge.

"I want it here," he agrees.

My dress rides up indecently high, and he's

pressed between my thighs. Every inch of me lives for the feeling of his body on mine.

But it's dangerous.

I've survived this long, kept myself focused, because I haven't let myself give in to the desire to touch him, to have him touch me.

"Come on, Six. Don't back out now." His voice is a low murmur.

I take a breath and thread my fingers through his hair, tugging him closer. Our lips hover close enough to touch, and I'm aching for him, the need pulsing low in my stomach wanting to drop us out of this bar, out of this city, to a place where it's him and me and everything we've never said.

I can't close the last millimeter between us.

As if he knows, Tyler does it for me.

*Oh, God.*

I'd thought I remembered what it felt like to kiss him, but I was wrong.

He's warm and firm, heat and desire, and the second he parts my mouth with his tongue, I sigh against him.

It's supposed to be my kiss, but Tyler's fingers tangle in my hair, tilting my head as if he can't stand to sit back. His other hand finds my hip, angling me against the pool table so he can press closer to my center, forcing my legs apart.

He kisses me like he owns me, like he misses me, like he never wants to let me go.

My fingertips trail through his hair, my thighs squeezing as if I can entice him into me.

I want him in me. God, if he shifted me up onto this pool table right now, slid inside me and claimed me in front of this entire room, I wouldn't say no.

I don't know how long our hungry lips hitch and slide, our greedy hands touch and tease, but I tear my mouth away first, leaning my forehead against him while I struggle to catch my breath.

"Remember that guitar you bought me in high school?" he murmurs against my lips.

I nod, my throat too swollen to answer.

His hands skim up my sides, thumbs resting under the curve of my breasts as if they have every right to be there, as if I'm the instrument built for his hands.

Tyler's head turns a fraction of an inch so his lips brush the corner of my mouth. His next four words, whispered against my skin like a brand, stop my heart.

"I want it back."

**11**

# Annie

The rest of the weekend, I'm a bundle of nervous energy—practicing with Tyler and alone.

Because of the tight timeline, we're all business. Every minute, from dawn until midnight, we write and rewrite, play and sing, go over every section of my vocals and his guitar until the result is real and powerful and moves me from the first chord.

Monday morning, I can barely listen during Entertainment Management, my stomach flipping over as I stare off into space and go over the arrangement in my head.

On my way out of class, I notice a missed call from Haley, plus a voicemail.

*Annie, we sent you flowers for midterms, but the florist couldn't deliver them because there was no one with your name at the dorm address you gave us. I told them to try again, but here's the number—*

I write down the number, then hang up on the voicemail.

This is bad.

I call the florist, who's super confused and asks if there's another address to deliver to.

I don't want to give her the Vanier one, so I go down to the shop and get them myself, calling my dad on the way back.

"Hey," I say when he answers, panting as I take the steps up from the subway, the big arrangement of purple orchids and roses heavy in my arms. "I got the flowers. Thank you, guys, that was very sweet."

"The florist said they couldn't deliver them." I can hear him frown over the phone.

"It was a mix-up. Everything's fine. There's actually something else I wanted you to send me." I tell him, and he pauses.

"If we send it to the same address, it'll arrive."

"For sure," I tell him.

After hanging up, I text Pen to remind her I gave her dorm as my address and that if someone happens to show up with a package, she should sign for me.

"It's a little early for congratulations flowers. You haven't even auditioned," Rae points out from her desk chair as I push open our door.

"They're from my dad and stepmom. The card says, 'Good luck on midterms!'" I set the arrangement on my desk, still wrapped, and Heath swims to the glass to check it out.

I drop onto the bed, pressing the heels of my hands to my eyes. "*Fuck*, I'm an asshole."

"Not the usual response to flowers."

I roll onto my side to look at her. "My dad doesn't know about... the showcase."

"Parents don't need to know everything," Rae says, folding her arms. "Mine don't."

"You never talk about your family. You're not close?"

Her dark brows lift. For a moment, I think she's not going to answer, but she does. "My parents are both doctors. So's my brother. They're not thrilled I'm here. I told them it's better here than Ibiza, where I spent last summer."

"You were never tempted to be what they wanted? Or to pretend?"

Rae opens her notebook computer in front of

her. "I'm not gonna tell someone else's story. I'm going to be the biggest DJ in the world. And every person who thinks that's not true gets to be wrong about me."

An expression of sheer determination crosses her face, and I can't help being inspired by her resolve.

"This sounds stupid and self-centered," I start, "but did I do something to make you not like me? Because I really wish we could start over."

She shifts in her seat. "Just because I like my space and my resting bitch face is on point doesn't mean I hate you. I mean... I fed your fish the other day."

"Really?"

Rae shrugs. "He looked hungry."

That lightens my heart. "Thank you."

"For what?"

"For being you."

She shakes her head before turning back to her computer, but I swear there's a trace of a smile on her lips too. "Whatever. What time's your audition?"

I check my phone. *Shit.* "In an hour. I need to go warm up."

I get off the bed, grab my things and start for the door.

I'm halfway down the hall when I hear her call, "If you fuck it up, I'm sending the flowers back."

———————

He's not here.

I'm in the grand auditorium twenty minutes before our scheduled time, and Tyler's nowhere to be seen.

I call him, text him, but nothing.

I pace in the hall until the door cracks and an admin assistant sticks her head out. "Mr. Adams?"

"That's me."

"You're on deck." She looks at me dubiously but lets me inside.

I head in the back door and into the wings as the current performer, a pianist, continues his audition.

"Next. Tyler Adams." The disembodied voice comes through a microphone.

Wiping sweaty palms on my pants, I take the stage.

A panel of adjudicators sits half a dozen rows back, representing each of the faculties. Their faces are familiar—Talbot, Finn, the dean, plus a man whose name I don't know who's a classical music teacher.

"Miss Jamieson," Talbot observes tightly. "You're not on our list. What are you doing here?"

"Tyler and I are auditioning together."

The judges exchange looks.

"Where is Mr. Adams?" the dean asks.

My stomach twists as silence falls over the auditorium.

The thought that rises up is involuntary, and awful.

*He left. He left again.*

When I'm about to open my mouth, the doors of the auditorium burst open, and Tyler strides in, guitar on his back.

"I'm sorry to keep you waiting," he says loudly enough the judges can hear too as he makes his way up the aisle. "One of our first-floor neighbors was broken into, and he cut himself on the glass. I called 9-1-1 and got him into an ambulance."

My jaw slackens. "Is he okay?"

"I think so."

"We'll give you a few minutes to warm up," the dean decides, turning to the admin assistant. "Let's get the next person, please."

I shut my eyes, heart still hammering as we head back to the wings together and a ballerina crosses our path for the stage.

Tyler squeezes my shoulders. "I wouldn't leave you," he murmurs, reading my expression. "I won't. Not again."

I study him, the nerves warring with gratitude in my body as he quietly tunes his guitar.

"Mr. Adams," a voice calls moments later when the dancer finishes. "Are you ready?"

We take the stage, and the dean nods. "Miss Jamieson, you can accompany Mr. Adams, but if you make the showcase, you won't be credited for the performance. It would be unfair to the freshman students who were not permitted to audition."

Before I can argue, Tyler's on it. "She's not my backup. She wrote the song. She's in this every bit as much as I am, and if you won't let her audition, I'm not auditioning either."

Could my heart expand any more?

My gaze trains on the four adjudicators.

"I say we let them do it. If it's not good enough, we say no," Finn weighs in.

"All right," the dean decides.

I turn and close the distance between Tyler and me. He gives me a nod of encouragement.

"Thank you," I murmur so only we can hear before returning to take my place at the other mic.

The song is magic.

I don't need to watch the faces in the audience, because in my heart, it's not for them. It's for us.

Our performance is a blend of who we were, who we are, who we're becoming—the imperfect synergy of Tyler and me and what we could create together.

It's poetry. Every lie, every struggle, every moment, makes sense in this instant.

When we're done, the stone-faced adjudicators tell us we'll hear back as early as tonight.

I trip off stage after Tyler, and as he sets down his guitar in front of him, I leap onto his back, throw my arms around his neck.

"That was so good," I pant in his ear, loving the feel of his warm, hard body under mine as he catches my legs.

He chuckles. "You were great."

I drop off his back, and he turns to face me. "*You* were great," I echo because I can't find other words.

Now, staring at him, the emotion slams into

me. "What you did for me today," I start, "what you risked..."

"You're worth it," he murmurs.

I'm thinking about that kiss Saturday night. From the way his eyes darken, so is he.

"What are you doing now?" he asks.

I groan. "I have a sociology assignment to finish for tomorrow, then Elle and I got free tickets to the symphony tonight."

"Keep your phone on."

I sigh out a breath of excitement. "Yeah."

He shoots me a look that's pure wanting, and my entire body tingles as he strokes a thumb down my cheek before turning to lead the way out of the auditorium.

It's so good, and not nearly enough.

---

"That better be a booty call," Elle whispers over the symphony.

I flip my phone to hide the light in the darkened theater. "I'm waiting for the showcase results," I whisper back.

I don't want to be that asshole interrupting a public event, but I'm waiting for the biggest news of my life.

All of the emotional turmoil I've felt this semester I put into five minutes with Tyler. Four choruses. Three verses. One bridge.

The symphony orchestra is amazing, *The Planets* a work of art, but I'm fidgeting, picking at the hem of my black dress.

When it's done, we applaud, then I hit refresh again.

"It's here!" I say hoarsely as the email subject line imprints on my brain.

The patrons in the next several seats look over.

I scan for my name or his. A breath whooshes out when I finish.

"Well?" Elle demands.

Emotion wells up in my chest, and I shake my head. "We didn't get in."

She sighs. "I'm sorry."

"No, I mean, we didn't only get in. We're closing the show. Me and Tyler."

I hold up the phone so she can see both our names.

Her face splits into a grin. "Damn."

I scan our row and the one behind, recognizing a couple dozen Vanier students. Since we're at intermission, I race out of the row and sprint to the subway.

I debate texting Tyler, but this requires a face-to-face conversation.

My fingers drum the pole until the doors open at his stop. I bound up the stairs, and the city lights blend with the throbbing in my gut.

These aren't the heels for sprinting, so I half jog, half limp down the street to Tyler's. In the dark, there're a few sketchy-looking people, but they can't crush my high. I ignore them, ignore everything until I'm under the streetlight in front of his building.

I hit the intercom, the buzzer ringing on the other end.

No answer.

I take off toward Vanier. I'm going to have serious blisters from these shoes, but within minutes, the familiar building looms over me, graceful and stately in the dark.

The glass doors give under my hands, the light of the hallways beyond. My feet ache, and my lungs burn, and I don't know what I'm running toward until a hoarse voice from down the hall has me grinding to a halt.

"Annie."

He's dressed in the same clothes as earlier, and he fills the hall despite the trickle of students moving past him. His face is full of emotions—maybe the same ones I'm feeling that create this impossible expansion in my chest.

Tyler closes the distance between us.

"You weren't at home," I say as he comes to a stop inches away.

"I was looking for you." His chest isn't heaving like mine, but his eyes are wild.

I must look like a mess, my hair sticking to my neck and face, my skin flushed. He doesn't seem to notice as his mouth curves with the ghost of a smile. "Congrats."

I muster a cocky smile. "Was there ever any doubt?"

He shakes his head, then before I can protest, he wraps his arms around my waist.

*He's going to kiss me.* Every nerve ending in my body tingles as I stare at his mouth. My hands land on his chest, and my eyes drift closed.

A moment later, my eager lips brush his cheek as he tugs me into a hard hug.

"Oh," I blurt. "Um. Thanks." I try too late for an awkward recovery.

I almost think I've gotten away with it when his

chest rumbles with laughter. "What did you think I was gonna do?"

"This," I lie, my fingers still trapped against his pecs. "Exactly this."

But I can't bring myself to care about the embarrassment, because being enveloped in his strength feels like home. His hand slides around my neck, fingers tangling in my hair.

I melt against him.

God, it's good to be in his arms.

When he pulls back an inch, our lips are a breath apart.

"I could kiss you now," he murmurs, and my heart skips. "You'd kiss me back, too," he continues in that beautiful voice. His mouth moves to brush my ear, lips skimming my skin and sending shivers through me.

"You seem extraordinarily confident," I manage.

Students pass us, but I don't know if they're looking. I'm trapped in Tyler's attention.

His chest is heat and muscle beneath my hands, and my fingers flex on his pecs through his thin shirt.

Tyler turns his face, lips grazing mine when he speaks. "A man who's seen heaven is more dangerous than one who only believes. And I'll never forget how it feels to have you need me."

My fingers dig into his muscled arms. I want him so much I ache.

I cut a look past him to the students in the hallway, the ones who don't know that everything in my life has been leading to this moment. Not only because of the showcase, but because of the man holding me.

"You don't have to remember it." I take a deep breath, ready to dive off the cliff. "I need you now."

12

# *Annie*

Tyler's kissing me.

He's dark and warm and thrilling, and when his tongue presses against my lips, I welcome him inside. It feels as if all I've ever wanted is to have him inside me—though I often think I'm part of him instead.

I'm the stars, burning and shifting, and Tyler's my sky, the dark and velvet eternity I live for.

If tonight hasn't already changed me, I know now that it will.

Tyler's steel arms bring my hips against his.

He's a brick wall, hard and unrelenting, and I want every inch of him.

Catcalls go up from somewhere.

Tyler pulls back, his breath rough, his gaze

liquid desire. I thread my fingers in his hair, grinning.

"What's that face?" he demands.

"That night we danced together, I decided your hair wasn't long enough to pull. I'm glad I was wrong."

His growl sends heat pooling between my thighs. "Upstairs. Now."

We stumble toward the stairwell, and the door closes after us.

"Please tell me Rae and Elle aren't home." He takes the steps two at a time. I try to keep up, my fingers laced with his.

"Don't think so." I hope to hell Elle's still at the performance and Rae's... wherever she disappears to.

On six, we trip down the hall, passing only one other girl on the way to my room, who offers me a thumbs up as she takes us in.

I push open the door, relieved to find it empty, then I tug my hand from his and head for my closet.

I take a ballet flat and hang it on the door handle. "It's not a sock, but she'll figure it out." I shut the door after us.

The laughter fades from his face, replaced by

intensity as he realizes the same thing as I do.

It's been five years since I had a crush on Tyler.

Two since I fell in love with him.

A year and a half since he broke my heart.

And now we're going to do this.

Tyler backs me toward the bed until my calves hit the side.

I'm older now. Wiser. This doesn't mean I'm losing my head or my heart.

But as he reaches behind his head and strips off his shirt, tossing it on the floor by the bed, I nearly swallow my tongue.

His shoulders are broader than I remember, his abs and pecs even more defined. Tyler's so distractingly attractive with clothes on it should be illegal for him to take them off.

"Holy... You're like art," I blurt, and his sudden smile cracks the mask of intensity on his face.

He's muscled and beautiful, and I want to trace my hand over every inch of him, especially when those muscles leap under my touch. But the ink swirling up his shoulder, across the left half of his chest, brings back a tiny portion of my brain power and has me questioning something beyond how it would feel to have his body over mine, driving into me.

"What are these?" I murmur, tracing the lines as he holds himself over me.

One looks like a flower over his pec, which connects to the vines down his arm. One beneath it looks like an old-fashioned ship rocked by waves. Farther down his ribs is a compass.

Tyler rasps out a breath. "You wanna do this now?"

He's testy and turned on, but I can't help myself. "Yes."

He inches back so I can bend to inspect him.

"This one, I got this one after I came to New York." He points to the ship. "This one after I started at Vanier." The compass. "This one this summer." The flower.

I bite my lip. "Tell me what they mean."

"Later. Turn."

I do as he asks, and he lifts my hair, laying it over one shoulder. His touch grazes between my shoulder blades, finding the zipper and working it down.

"The ink I want to hear about is all the words you wrote me on this." He strokes a finger across my skin, and I shiver.

Cool air hits my back as the straps slide off my

shoulders. The dress skims down my body, falling to the floor.

Tyler's lips graze my ear from behind. "Show me where you put me."

My entire body is humming when he turns me back to face him, and his expression strips away the rest of my defenses.

He's gorgeous. A fiery prince set out to claim what's his.

I point to my wrist. "Here."

He lifts it, presses an open-mouthed kiss to the skin there, and I shiver.

"And here." My finger brushes my stomach, next to my navel.

Tyler's hands smooth down my sides, and he bends, his lips hot on my stomach. I grab his hair as I swallow, the feeling of his wet mouth sending need pooling between my thighs.

"Don't stop now." His voice is barely audible.

I point to the inside of my thigh. "Here."

With a dark look, he drops to his knees.

Then he strokes a finger up my skin, close to my panties.

I sway.

I want him to touch me. I need it more than air.

He bends toward my center, my panties the

only thing between his mouth and where I'm slowly burning up.

His lips graze my skin on the inside of my thigh. "Every word you wrote I'll trace with my tongue."

It's too much. I'm overwhelmed.

But before I can respond, he rises and steps away, nodding at my bra and panties. "Take them off."

He says it softly—a question, not a command—but the fact that he's asking makes it impossible to deny him. With shaking hands, I reach for the back of the bra and unhook it. It slides down my arms and falls to the floor. Swallowing, I hook my fingers in my panties and slide them down too.

When I straighten, my knees are shaking. It's only when his finger finds my chin, tilting it up, that I realize I was staring at his feet.

"It's just me," he murmurs.

"I know." My lips curve, wavering. "That's why I'm shaking."

An expression of hunger and utter adoration fills his face. His hand finds my hip, tugs me close to him. "Me too."

He presses himself between my thighs, and my eyes squeeze shut. The roughness of his jeans sends waves of sensation through me. Tyler's hands slide up my sides. He palms my breasts as if they're precious, as if I am. The callouses on his fingers feel so good and a little dirty.

I arch into him, wrapping my fingers around his neck and pressing my lips to his shoulder. He responds, rolling one of my nipples between his thumb and finger.

Ribbons of pure pleasure shoot between my thighs. "Oh God."

He switches to the other breast, and the tugging between my thighs intensifies, grows from a thread of desire to a chain of need—need for this, for him, for more.

"You feel so good in my hands. The times I've wanted to do this, Six, just this…"

My fingers dig into his neck, urging him to continue, but he nods at the bed.

I shift back onto the comforter, and he follows me, then moves down my body. When I realize where he's headed, his name tumbles from my lips.

"I've come so many times thinking of you," I whisper.

He rubs the back of his hand across his mouth. "You're about to again."

*Holy.*

Tyler drags my ankles apart.

I want this, but I'm too exposed. I try to close my legs, and he looks up, darkly questioning.

He doesn't correct me. Instead, he traces a path down my stomach with his fingers, and right before they dip where I need them, they turn, stroking the inside of one shaking thigh.

My thighs spread on their own—an inch, then another.

His touch traces up the other thigh, but it's too slow and too soft. I bite my lip in frustration.

He brushes across my opening, and I buck my hips.

"You're so wet," he growls, his fingers returning to toy with me. "The things we could do with you this wet."

I'm so close to whining, to fucking begging him to touch me. Maybe he knows and likes it.

"Tell me you want it," Tyler murmurs. "Ask me with those pretty words. That voice I can't get out of my head."

I shift up on my elbows, my heart hammering in my chest as I stare down at him. "Tyler Adams. I've been waiting years for you to fuck me. *Do it already.*"

His chocolate eyes flash with heat and satisfaction before he lowers his head. His tongue hits the sweet spot between my thighs, and it's like being jolted with an electric current.

Oh. My. God.

My head falls back against the covers as need, hot and wet, rushes over me.

He moves between the lightest touch of his tongue and slow strokes with his finger as if I'm an instrument he's experimenting with for the first time.

My hips snap toward him. My hands fist in the sheets.

"More," I pant, writhing, but he ignores me.

Just when I'm starting to get into a rhythm with his mouth, his damn finger takes its place, teasing and stroking, pressing inside an inch only to slip back out.

"Tyler..."

He takes pity on me, sliding that finger all the way in. The feeling is exquisite, and it's only his damned hands.

I grab his hair and exhale hard.

If I'd ever wanted to know how Tyler got to be so good at music, it's obvious from the way he pleasures me.

Every touch and stroke is an experiment that informs the next, one that he changes and repeats and twists into a pattern that drives me insane with need.

But I'm learning him, too, learning how to make him give me what I want.

Like saying his name.

By the time he's sucking on my skin in earnest, sliding a second finger into me, I'm making noises with every breath.

I squirm because I can't not, and that makes him groan. "All the times I got off to you, I never thought you'd be this tight. I don't know if I could have stayed away."

Those filthy words have me breaking on his lips, my hands fisting in his hair as I arch against him, crying out his name.

The last thing I see before my eyes squeeze shut is his face, full of need and satisfaction.

I ride out the waves of feeling with him, on him.

When the aftershocks rock me, he slows but doesn't pull back. He licks me clean, as if every inch of me was made for his enjoyment and he won't allow any of it to go to waste.

"Wow," I murmur, dragging him up my body so

I can loop my arms around his neck. "At the risk of inflating your ego," I start, and his mouth, still wet from me, curves. "You're pretty good at that."

"Pretty good." Tyler brushes his lips across mine, and I can taste myself on him. It's the sexiest thing I've ever experienced.

"Let's see what else you're good at."

My hands drop to the button on his jeans, hovering there as I take in this moment. Him and me. Joined.

For real.

*Fucking finally.*

But his hand closes over mine.

"Tell me you're going to fuck me already," I murmur.

Tyler brushes a piece of hair out of my face, his tight jaw working.

"No. I'm not."

13

—————

# *Tyler*

The last time I kissed Annie Jamieson in her bed was eighteen months ago. We were different people then.

I'm reminded how different as her eyes flash up at me.

"What the hell?" Annie demands. She's naked and beautiful and, apparently, pissed.

I roll off her and onto my back. I can still taste her, and the way she fell apart under my hands and mouth left me nowhere near satisfied, but I force out the words I need to say. "Tonight was about you. Giving you what I wanted to give you then."

"You're overthinking this." She shifts over me, and I bite back the groan at the feel of her. "Stop thinking. Just be here with me. I know you want to."

She's killing me—with her voice and her intentions and the way she responds. My cock is swollen and leaking at the thought of making her mine.

But the second I make her mine, I'm hers, too. And even though I want her back, I'm grasping for some semblance of control.

She's so fucking sweet, with a new edge I love every bit as much as the sweetness.

Unable to resist, I prop myself up on my elbows and tug her lips down to mine. My fingers tangle in her silky hair, wrapping it around my hand like I've been thinking about all semester until she opens over me.

I used to tease Annie Jamieson for wearing her heart on her sleeve, but I feel as if I'm the one who's exposed.

I want to bury myself inside her so deep she can't get me out. Not now, not ever.

Her breasts graze my bare chest, making my impatient dick swell even more. This time when her hands drop to the button on my jeans, I don't stop her.

Not when she works the zipper down, makes a little groan in her throat as she sees the hard ridge of my cock, the wet spot on my boxer briefs.

Not when she reaches inside, her aroused gaze meeting mine.

My eyes fall shut as her hand wraps around my shaft. Her touch is warm and soft and a cruel tease. I want to be inside her yesterday.

"Holy fuck, Six." I whisper it like a prayer.

She helps me work my jeans off. I get up long enough to find a condom from my wallet and roll it on while she watches, breathless.

"Wait," she murmurs when I shift over her again.

I laugh softly. "You were the one so anxious to do this."

"But I want to savor it, too."

I can't speak.

So, I kiss her instead as I wedge myself between her soft thighs.

I nudge her opening, groaning into her mouth because she's so hot and wet.

Every part of me pulses as I press inside an inch at a time.

I watch her face, see her eyes go dark as she gasps when I fill her.

*There's my girl.*

*Mine now. Always.*

"You okay?" I ask when I'm halfway inside her.

She nods, swallowing. She's tight and hot and slick and perfect.

"I know. It's a lot to take in," I say.

Her hand slaps my chest, and I grin as I bend to kiss her again.

Her panting breaths mingle with mine as I sink all way in. My head drops back as the feel of what we're doing overtakes me.

When she wraps her legs around me, urging me to move, I shake my head. "We gotta go slow, or I'm going to lose control."

"I don't want slow, and I don't want you in control." She licks lips swollen from my kisses. "I want to free-fall."

*Fuck.* I can't hold back when she talks like that.

When I sink back inside her, she arches her back to meet me, her face transformed with desire.

I want to give her so much pleasure she can't come without thinking of me.

Every stroke is a memory I need to preserve. She's tight and soft, and I could explore the contradiction forever.

Except that tonight we've got somewhere to be.

I've waited for this girl for years, and I'm not waiting another second.

I build her up, toeing the line between deliberate and reckless. This might be our first time together, but I know her. I know how she thinks, how she feels, what emotions make her lips tremble and her eyes glow.

Tonight, I'm going to learn how to make her scream.

My mouth claims hers, swallowing every sound and breath. I'm greedy for all of her, any of her, and I won't let a single element of her reaction go to waste.

Annie's hips lift to meet mine, and I lift her higher so I'm in control, so I can go deeper.

I tear my lips from hers to drag them down her jaw, the long, beautiful neck she's offering up.

"Oh my God. Oh my God. Oh my God."

Her chants spur me on.

*We're in this together, Six. You and me.*

When she squeezes around me, her nails digging into my skin as she moans my name...

I die.

I swear my heart stops.

I never want to spend a moment on this planet without knowing that expression of delirious pleasure on her face, without having it imprinted on my mind, in my soul.

I will destroy any man who even thinks about her like this.

I can't hold back. I come. It's everything I ever dreamed and some things I wouldn't dare.

I pulse for fucking ages, my abs clenching as I try to think of a way I can stay inside her like this forever because nothing will ever be as good as this moment.

When we come down, I reluctantly roll us so she's on top because I don't want to crush her.

We lie like that, me stroking her hair and staring at the faded white ceiling, until something buzzes near my head.

Annie twists, moving off me to grab her phone from the nightstand. "It's Rae. She saw the shoe, but she needs to get into the room."

I force my languid body off the bed, grabbing a box of tissues to clean up.

My attention lands on a vase of flowers. "Nice gift. Should I be jealous?"

"It's from Dad and Haley."

"You gotta tell them." I try for casual, but Annie stiffens anyway as she tugs a long T-shirt over her head.

I might not have earned the right to tell her what to do, but she must see how futile keeping her education from him is, how much worse she's making it with every day she puts it off.

"I will when I'm ready." She narrows her gaze. "I liked your mouth better twenty minutes ago."

"I'm sure you did." I step closer, watch her eyes darken as I do. I want to kiss her again, but I'm afraid if I start, I'll never leave.

My gaze lands on something—a fishbowl next to the flowers—and I cock my head. "Was he watching us the whole time?"

"Heath? Probably, but he's pretty judgy. You guys would get along great."

I muss her hair in retaliation, and she ducks away, grinning.

I cross toward the door, then pull the door open and hold out the shoe.

She takes it from me and taps it against her hand.

When I don't move, Annie raises a brow. "You waiting for me to say, 'Thank you for the orgasms. I'll study so much better now'?"

"My ego would appreciate that."

"Fine. That was very relaxing."

"Relaxing?" I echo, closing in on her. "Don't

pretend you're not rubbing one out to me in the shower later."

She reaches up to wind her arms around my neck, pressing her body against mine. I'm already getting hard again at the feel of her soft curves.

"Feels like you miss me already."

I bite back the groan, my eyes narrowing. "I'm going to make you beg, Six."

Annie's lips part, her breath mingling with mine. "Promise?"

She pulls back before I can decide whether to leave or drag up that T-shirt and fuck the smug smile off her lips.

With a last look, I head down the hall, pulling the door closed after me.

*I do miss her already.* But not the way she means.

***

"You're home late," Beck comments from the living room when I unlock the door of our apartment.

I kick off my shoes and toss my wallet on the counter. "We're closing the showcase. Me and Annie. The schedule gets announced publicly tomorrow."

Beck's face splits into a grin. He descends on me, clapping me on the back.

"You deserve it, Ty. The break. The stage. The girl," he says meaningfully as he crosses to the couch and flicks on the TV. "You should look happier."

I grab a beer from the fridge.

"I am happy, but people say that like you've arrived. Like getting what you want is a destination. Those moments don't last, Beck." I think of my dad, what he went through—how entitled he felt, how quickly anything he found slipped through his fingers.

"You want certainty, you're in the wrong business, my friend," Beck says.

I join my roommate on the couch. "Music."

"Life."

The TV's on silent but playing some reality show.

"*Smackdown*," he reminds me. "The contestants put themselves through these insane physical tests to try to win a bunch of money. Mostly they end up with bruises, sometimes broken bones, and nothing to show for it."

"That's messed up."

"We do exactly the same thing." He reaches for

my beer with a smirk and takes a long drink before passing it back. "When I met you last fall, I knew you were walking around this city with a broken heart. When Annie showed up this year, the pieces clicked into place. But instead of thanking whatever god you pray to for giving you another chance, you're thinking of all the reasons it won't work."

"Last time, neither of us knew what we wanted. We were kids, Beck, playing at being grown-ups. We've both changed. We have more than dreams —we have plans. But I lost myself in her, and it took walking away to realize it."

Beck cocks his head. "Are you in love with her?"

"I don't know if I ever fell out of love with her."

The words settle between us, my abs contracting as my mind takes me back to her dorm room an hour ago. I'd barely finished touching her before I wanted to touch her again.

"Seeing her again this fall, it's like a part of me I thought was dead came back to life. And more of me came with it, a part that helped my music and made me feel more alive than I have in a year. She always got me like no one else, and even when I wouldn't let her in, she'd find her way.

"When I tried to work for Zeke, he said some-thing was missing. She brings something out of me that's not there when she's gone."

"One thing I can't figure out is why she's here. Why doesn't she get her dad to set her up with a contract?"

"Because she wants to build her own castles. I respect the hell out of that."

Beck's eyes gleam. "Girl's got you thinking about the future, huh?"

He's pushing my buttons on purpose, but the thought of a future with her has me aching. "She's like a song. She can be across the country, but I hear her name, or see someone who looks like her, or read something that sounds like she wrote it, and in a moment, she's back. I'm dropped into this world of feeling, trapped in the same place. And I don't want to leave.

"The stakes now are higher than ever. But even if I know there's a chance of breaking her heart or her breaking mine and ruining both our lives... I want her too much to walk away."

"Then don't."

We turn back to the TV, where middle-aged contestants are racing through an obstacle course built over a pool to try to win a car.

When a balding man slips on a moving disc and tumbles into the water with a massive splash, I say, "I thought we were supposed to get smarter when we get older."

Beck holds out a hand for my beer again, and I pass it to him. "Propaganda."

# 14

# Annie

"You're quiet for someone who landed a spot closing the showcase," Elle points out at breakfast. "It's mind sex, isn't it?"

I blink, ripping off a piece of my untouched bagel. "You mean fantasizing?"

"Don't make it sound pretty. It's hot and dirty, and you're doing it."

Rae drops into a seat next to us with her coffee, surprising both of us. "It wasn't mind sex that kept me out of my room Monday night."

It's true, and for the last thirty-six hours, all I've been able to think about is Tyler.

Not the showcase we landed, but the things I want to do with Tyler that have nothing to do with music and everything to do with his hands and mouth and body.

Yesterday, we agreed to spend the day catching up on our schoolwork before launching back into rehearsing.

Still, we ran into each other accidentally-on-purpose in the halls at school, and he pulled me into a stairwell for a hot and too-short make-out.

If we hadn't both had class to go to, I know we would've ended up in my room again.

I want that so badly.

In some ways, it's a good thing Tyler and I never sealed the deal in high school. Neither of us would've graduated.

My phone rings, interrupting my daydream, and I answer without looking.

"Annie Jamieson?" the warm female voice asks.

I straighten, but Elle and Rae don't seem to be listening. "Yes."

"This is Kelly Fox from Lighthouse Representation. I saw the schedule for the Vanier showcase online."

My mind spins with a million questions at once —how she found me, how she got my number, but most of all, *The showcase lineup is posted online?*

Of course it is.

But if it was so easy for her to get it, will my dad see it?

My stomach twists as she goes on. "I assume you're Annie Jamieson, daughter of Jax Jamieson. I wanted to talk to you about your options for representation."

"You're an agent." My heart thuds.

Elle's and Rae's gazes snap to me.

"Are you calling Tyler Adams too?" I press.

I don't miss the pause before she answers. "Annie, we have to be selective about our clients."

Indignation rises up. "You need to talk to Tyler." I take a breath. "Whatever you think I can do for you, he can do more. Come to the show. You won't be disappointed."

I hang up.

"Why would you pass on an agent?" Elle demands.

"I didn't pass," I reply before realizing I sort of did. "She should've been interested in Tyler."

"She could've been interested in *both* of you."

I frown. "Maybe. But it didn't sound like it." I spot a familiar person heading into the dining hall and wave.

Beck flips a chair around and sits astride it, grinning. "Morning, ladies."

"Tyler's not with you, is he?" I cut a look toward the doors.

"Nope."

"Good." Determination sets in. "I need you to send an email to Zeke's studio with the schedule for the showcase. Tell him Kelly Fox called asking about Tyler and you wanted to do him the courtesy of letting him know people are sniffing around."

His gaze narrows as if he's trying to figure out what I'm up to. "My boy know about this?"

"No. And you're not going to tell him."

"I'm not in the habit of keeping secrets from my roomie," he warns.

"This is for him," I promise.

After breakfast we go to Entertainment Management, where I take notes through our guest lecturer's presentation.

Next it's Talbot's class.

She checks in on the status of our term project: a monologue that blends a piece of cinema with our own inspiration.

I've jotted down some ideas, but I've been so focused on the showcase I haven't progressed further. Maybe it has something to do with the fact that of all my professors, she's the only one who seems to go out of her way to cut me down.

Elle leans over while Talbot discusses the assignment with one of our classmates. "I heard she's writing a musical," my friend murmurs.

I nearly drop my pen. "Seriously?"

"Yeah. You know she acted on Broadway on and off for like two decades."

"I remember reading that. But I had no idea she wrote, too."

I can't reconcile our tough professor with the type of person I always imagined penning for the stage, but I can't let it go.

After class, I approach her. "Miss Talbot? I heard you're writing a musical. Can you tell me about it?"

She straightens, staring at me for an extra-long beat as if looking for something new. "I'm writing the book—the lyrics," she goes on. "My writing partner does the score." She gathers up her books from the desk and starts to brush past me when I call after her.

"I love musicals. I know Broadway doesn't have the money Hollywood does or the tradition of Shakespeare, but musical theater is big and bright and raw and unapologetic and honest... There's nothing else that can make you cry and laugh in the same three minutes. Or that can make your heart expand until you swear it's going to burst out of your ribs. It's the most beautiful, unapologetically human form of expression I've ever seen."

I'm being more candid with her than I've been all year, but it's too late to change that.

She turns back. Her lips purse and I brace myself, waiting for her to bite out something harsh.

Instead she says, "My partner and I have an off-Broadway show running right now."

When she gives me the name, I write it down immediately. "I'll go see it this weekend."

Her lips twitch at the corner. "If you're that interested, I can have a couple of seats for you Friday at will call."

By the time I dash out of class to head over to the Columbia campus to study with Pen, I'm already feeling bouncier than I have in weeks.

---

That night in my room, I text Tyler, triumphant.

. . .

Annie: I scored us a practice room for tomorrow. You can thank me now or later.

The response comes back almost immediately.

Tyler: I can do us one better if you're willing to go to Brooklyn.

Annie: ???

Tyler: I'm playing a session gig for Zeke. We'll probably finish early, and we can use the studio for a bit if so.

Thursday after class at Columbia, I have lunch with Pen, catching up on both of our gossip. According to her eyebrows plastered to her hairline, I've won this round.

Before I leave campus, she hands me the oversized package that was delivered to her room with my name on it.

It's perfect timing, and I take it on the subway with me to Brooklyn.

I use the map on my phone to find the brick building on the corner. Inside, the woman at the desk gets me an escort to studio two.

The producer acknowledges me with a nod through the glass panel in the door, and moments later, the door opens. I head into the booth as my attention's drawn to the guy on the other side of the glass.

Tyler's sitting on a stool, guitar in his lap, laughing with the other guys in the band.

He's so handsome and competent, perfectly at ease, and my chest expands as I watch him.

I'm proud of him but a little envious, too.

"They're wrapping up. I'm Zeke."

My head turns toward the fit, middle-aged man on this side of the glass wearing a sport coat with jeans.

"Annie." I hold out a hand.

His gaze narrows as he takes it. "Annie...?"

"Just Annie."

Tyler comes through the door. His eyes brighten with pleasure as he sees me.

"Nice work today, Tyler," Zeke says. "I might have a gig for you. You free Tuesday night?"

His brows lift. "What kind of gig?"

"The kind that you'd change anything in your calendar for." Zeke claps a hand on Tyler's shoulder. "It's at Madison Square Garden. I'll send you the details."

I think Zeke's going to leave, but his attention homes in on the guitar case at my side.

"If you wanted a different guitar, we could've gotten you one," he says, shaking Tyler's hand before disappearing out the door, leaving us alone.

I set the case next to the board and step back.

Tyler doesn't say anything as he flips the latches on the hardtop case, lifts the guitar, and hooks it over his head.

He tunes it before striking up a melody that's haunting at first, then switches to something lively and joyful, then ending with notes of tension and resolution.

It's breathtaking.

He sets the guitar back in its case, then drops into a chair, leaning back. His eyes darken. "Tell me something—were you ever tempted to return it?"

"Yeah," I half groan, half laugh. "For a while, it was all I wanted."

I reach for a chair of my own, but a restraint

closes around my wrist. I glance at Tyler's strong grip in surprise.

"I appreciate the guitar, Six. But it's not the only thing I want back."

I lift my chin, studying the intensity on his face. "I know."

He tugs me into his lap, and I don't fight it.

I drape an arm over the back of his chair, his hair brushing my hand.

His body is hard under me. I give in to the urge to trace my finger along his rounded shoulder, stop short of hooking it in the rounded collar and burying my face in his neck to absorb the scent of him like I want to. "We're here to practice," I point out, but my voice is low.

He pulls me closer, brushing the hair back behind my ear to drop kisses up my neck. "We will. But first, I'm saying thanks for the guitar."

My head drops back. "You're so"—I bite back a moan as his teeth find my earlobe, arching my ass against his crotch—"welcome."

God, I want him right here in this room, and from the hardness of him everywhere, he wants that too.

"So, first a studio and second a gig at MSG?" I pull back, try to focus on work.

Tyler resists, tracing a finger along my neck, making me bite my tongue. "Yeah. Zeke called me yesterday to say congrats on the showcase. I didn't even have to tell him. It's weird."

Around the haze of desire, I realize Beck's email must have worked. Zeke got wind people were sniffing around Tyler.

*Good.*

"I'm sure he realized what he was missing," I murmur, all innocence.

Tyler shifts me so I'm straddling him, and that only makes the need pulsing between my thighs worse. "Um... this is seriously distracting," I mumble even as I link my hands behind his head.

"I'm counting on it. That way you'll say yes when I tell you I want to take you out."

"How's tomorrow?" I ask, breathless.

His smile freezes as he cocks his head. "Honestly, I expected more pushback."

I laugh. "I have tickets to a musical my acting professor wrote. I'm actually kind of excited. I know people write musicals because obviously, for them to exist, someone needed to create them... but in my mind, those shows are timeless. The idea that someone"—I almost say "I" but stop—"could actually weave one from nothing is mind blowing. So, can you make it?"

"I need to head out of town this weekend for a personal thing," he says, regret coloring his voice.

Disappointment courses through me. I assume he means for his dad, and I squeeze his arm. "Sure. You want to talk about it?"

His expression softens. "Nah. But thanks for understanding."

I want him, and more than that, I care about him. There's still so much up in the air between us.

But it's hard to be caught up in that. It's hard to do anything but relax into his arms, surveying the room.

"Just think. In another year, you could be on contract. On tour," I say, even though the idea of him being gone tugs at my heart.

"You might have to come with me."

My stomach flips over. "You invite a girl on tour with you, that's serious," I warn.

His gaze searches mine, his hands tightening around me. "I know this showcase is everything to you. But it's not all that matters to me. Every time I picture my future, I think of you in it."

My heart squeezes as he leans in, brushing his mouth over mine. I kiss him back, putting all the words we haven't said into it until he pulls back an inch.

"You need to tell your dad you're here," Tyler murmurs against my mouth.

My head drops back. "I will. I don't know why it matters so much."

His expression. "I don't want this hanging over you."

I sigh, tracing a finger over his parted lips. I want them on me again. "It almost seems as if this is bothering you more than it's bothering me," I tease.

Tyler stiffens under me, but before he can respond, an alert on his phone has us both jumping.

"Thirty minutes," he curses. "We better work."

I'm already missing his warmth before he shifts me off him.

## 15

# Tyler

Showcase auditions might be over, but as the limo that picked me up at DFW pulls up Jax's driveway Saturday afternoon, I feel as if the real test is beginning.

As I step out of the car, a stinging breeze sweeps past, lifting the hairs on my arms despite my sweater and denim jacket.

When I reach the top of the familiar stairs, my fist hovers over the door, but before I can knock, it swings wide.

"Tyler!"

Haley's beaming face takes the edge off my nerves. When she opens her arms wide for a hug, I can't resist. Even though I'm bigger than her, it feels as if she's the one holding me.

"We were so glad you called."

"I know it was last minute," I say against her dark hair.

"Not at all. We live minute to minute around here. We have a guest bedroom ready for you tonight. I only wish you'd stay longer."

Something bumps against my legs, and I glance down. "Sophie?!"

A round face with amber eyes and dark hair peers up at me, breaking into a smile that's too big, too earnest, to belong to an actual human.

"Holy shit, she's big." I grimace as I realize what I've said.

"Jax says worse all the time. Soph, let Tyler in the door."

I follow them down the hall toward the kitchen. It feels comfortable and strange at once.

"You look fantastic," she says over her shoulder. "How long has it been?"

"Too long," I admit.

"I know we've kept in touch over the past year, but it's not the same as seeing you in person." She sighs. "Well, you're here now. Jax is sitting on the patio. I think he's trying to escape Sophie, who runs all over the house like a demon."

I glance at the tiny person in question, her face

all innocence. "We can't let him get away, can we?" I hoist her up, grunting as I shift her against my side. She laughs, delighted, as I head for the double doors.

"Want a beer?" Haley calls after me. "Or a bourbon?"

"I'm good. Thanks, Haley."

From the expression on her face, she knows I mean thanks for so much more than the drink offer. It's a thank-you for everything—for working with me back at Wicked, for letting me into her house two years ago, for letting me remain in their lives after the chaos I caused.

"You're family," she says before nodding at Sophie. "Go get Daddy."

"Get Daddy," Sophie repeats, and I grin.

We find Jax sitting in a patio chair by the glistening water.

"Daddy!" Sophie squeals, holding out her arms.

She scrambles out of my arms as I take a seat, but instead of climbing into her dad's lap, she runs circles around his chair and mine.

"When she was a baby, I thought, 'It'll be easier when she gets older,'" my mentor says in lieu of a greeting. "But they change. They don't get easier."

"Never?"

Jax meets my gaze for the first time. "Not when they start high school. Learn to drive. Or when they start a good college across the country. You ever think about her?" he asks.

The knot in my gut twists tighter. "All the time."

I wanted Annie to tell her dad for her own sake but also because of this eventuality—that I have to lie to her dad's face.

I'd do anything for her, but I hate this, especially when he goes on.

"It's hard not to have her around the house. When she first moved in, it surprised me every time I saw her or heard her. But the last couple years, I took for granted she was under my roof.

"When she was seven and still living with my sister, I learned Grace was getting bruises from her husband. I told her to leave him. She said it was under control.

"I tried to get out of my touring contract so I could get my kid—couldn't bring her on the road with me—but the head of my label wouldn't let me. I was already a big deal, and he threatened to sue my ass if I didn't finish up.

"It was the first time in my life I trashed a hotel

room. Broke all the furniture. I left the tour for three days to go see Annie and Grace. Grace promised me her husband never touched Annie. I hired someone to watch the house when I couldn't be there. Check on her at school, make sure she was okay."

"You didn't believe Grace."

"I believed her. But I wouldn't risk anyone, even my own sister, being wrong about the most precious thing in my life."

Jax's admissions swirl in my head. The year I went without Annie in my life sucked, but I didn't realize how much of the same Jax had endured— in the back of a tour bus, wanting nothing more than to get his kid, to make her safe, to make her his.

"I didn't know," I say at last.

He nods. "Before I met Haley, Annie was my entire fucking world. This industry tried to keep me away from her. I will always care what she's doing, and I will always want her to have the kind of freedom I didn't."

I turn that over. I get why he's protective, just like I get why she calls him overbearing.

I wish I could reconcile those because I care about both of them, but I can't.

"So, why're you here?" Jax prods finally.

"Zeke's been friendly the last week," I say, getting to the real reason for my visit. "I wondered if you had something to do with it."

Jax holds out a hand, and Sophie grabs onto his wrist, giggling as she tries to continue running her laps by dragging her dad with her. Neither Jax nor the chair moves an inch, even when she screeches.

"He might've called me to ask if I'd trust you enough for another shot."

"What'd you tell him?"

"Yes. Obviously."

"Thank you," I say and mean it. He waves me off.

"I know things weren't easy when you moved to New York. What happened to your dad... You could've fallen off the map. Instead, you went into your craft. I wish I'd done the same."

Gratitude washes over me, clashing with the guilt. I shouldn't be keeping secrets from this man. He's the closest thing I've had to a father.

But if Jax suspects something, he doesn't let on. "Talking to Zeke gave me a distraction from the legal headaches I've been dealing with."

I straighten in my seat. "So, you're still trying to

get your IP back from Wicked?" I recall the conversation we had over the summer, which was the last time we spoke on the phone.

"It's looking more and more unlikely." He grimaces. "Fuck studios. If I was starting over today, I'd start my own label. Not an outreach program like Big Leap. A real studio with clout."

I cock a brow. "Still could."

He stares at me as if I'm joking, a slow smile splitting his face. "You know, I don't spend much time wondering when I fucked up. But sending you away might've been one of those moments. I said I sent you away for you, for her. But it was for me too. I was afraid for you both."

My chest tightens at his words.

Sophie babbles at Jax's knee, and he scoops her up. But even as she presses her face to his chest, his serious eyes are on me.

"You remember Tyler," he murmurs to his daughter.

"Tire," she repeats evenly. There's no hesitation in it, no self-consciousness.

Kids have this way of being completely honest. They don't know how much pain the world can cause. They don't know what will be expected of them. I envy them.

"If you and Haley had met when you were starting out, do you think you two would've ended up together?" I ask.

Jax is quiet so long I think he's forgotten my question as he gazes toward the house. "I would love Haley in this lifetime or the next. I'd know her if I was deaf, dumb, and blind." His eyes crinkle at the corners. "I don't credit the universe with much, because I've built everything I have. But could I have fought for us like I did if we'd met at a different time, a different place? That I don't know."

I stare out over the pool. I think of our times here, the party Annie held for the musical, the night she brought me that guitar, a million nights in between.

I wanted us then, but maybe it wasn't our time.

*I want us now.* The truth of that rings through me.

But I can't be honest with Jax today, and as much as I hate that, I have to live with it. I care for him like he's my own father. This man is the only person I've leaned on when it comes to my music, my future.

But I care for Annie, too. Maybe it proves how much I care for her that I'm willing to risk not once, but twice what I have with him for that chance at something with her.

"I will never forget what you've done for me," I say at last.

Jax rubs a hand over his jaw, eyes glinting. "That sounds like an apology."

I don't answer.

He shifts out of his chair, hitching Sophie up on his hip. "You're staying for dinner."

It's a statement, not a question.

I've had some big moments in my life—ones that filled me up, made me feel like more than I am.

The gig at Madison Square Garden Tuesday night blows them out of the water.

"That was unreal," the bassist says, congratulating me in the wings after the show and clapping a hand on my shoulder. "You play it better than Randy."

I shake my head. "I'm sure your guitarist will be back in no time."

"Six to eight weeks to get the cast off," the lead singer comments as he passes us. "Could be six to eight months if we get to keep you in the meantime."

I take all of it in, grateful they gave me this shot and that it worked out, but I'm looking around for a familiar face.

I finally see her in the wings and take a minute to soak her in.

Annie looks gorgeous in tight black jeans and an off-the-shoulder top, her dark hair waving over her shoulders, but she could be wearing a bag for all I care. I'm so glad she's here.

"You were amazing!" she gushes, throwing her arms around me.

"I'm sweaty," I warn.

"You're perfect." The warmth in her voice cracks my chest.

I pull her against me because I need that mouth. It feels like a lifetime since I've had it, which is crazy because it's only been a few days.

Since I got back from Dallas on Sunday, we haven't had a chance to be alone together because of midterms and studying and the fact that either Beck or Rae and Elle seem to be swarming our rooms every second.

When I pull back, she looks dazed but recovers

fast. "Don't get the wrong idea. I'm not into rock stars."

I lean in until my lips brush her ear. "Glad to be your exception."

After the show, we hang out backstage with the band and our friends, sitting around a couch and chairs in the dressing room.

A bottle of champagne arrives with a card from Zeke, saying, "To the first of many."

Elle and Beck pop it while Annie retrieves me a beer.

"Since you hate champagne," she murmurs. I love that she remembers.

"But I don't hate you. Come here." I set the beer on the table and pull her into my lap on the couch.

Elle clears her throat, and it takes me a moment to realize everyone's watching us.

"We're gonna go find a bathroom," Elle says.

"All of us?" Beck echoes.

"Yeah, all of us." She grabs his arm. "We'll catch you guys outside later."

After they trail out of the room, I drop my head back against the couch.

"You were unbelievable," Annie murmurs. "It's

what I wanted for you. And it's only the beginning."

She bends to kiss me, but I hold her away.

I want to touch her and forget everything else, but... "There's something I have to say."

"Is this about where you went on the weekend?" Annie asks, her mouth pursing.

"Indirectly." I haven't told her I went to see her dad and Haley. It's not exactly a secret, but I know it would raise a bunch of questions, and I don't want to have that conversation right now or stress her out and make her think I might out her.

"My dad wanted to make it as a musician. He couldn't, and he blamed it on me. I've always been afraid of doing that to someone else. Of getting in so deep in a relationship I can't get out. Living with you and your dad and Haley? It was the first family I had. But your dad handed me an exit and... I'm not gonna say he told me to take it, because it's all on me.

"I wanted to be enough for you. I'm not yet. But I won't stop trying until I am."

Annie's hands slide down to my shoulders. From the expression on her face, I know she sees the way I feel about her.

"Tyler." Her throat works, and her voice has me aching to pull her closer. "You were always enough for me. Even when we were friends back in Philly. I'd never met anyone like you, and I never have since. You're kind and smart and so talented, but that's not what I see when I look at you. I see the way you care for people and look out for them. I see your heart. You try to protect it, and I get why, but you don't have to try so hard."

"No?" I can barely breathe, and she shakes her head.

"I'll protect it, too."

*Fuck.* This girl walks around trying to prove herself when just getting out of bed in the morning means she's enough.

I kiss her because I can't not kiss this girl—this woman, the one who's grown up under my gaze and when I wasn't looking.

"I'm going to tell my dad about the showcase," she says, pulling back. "And send him an invitation."

"Good." Relief washes over me. I didn't realize just how twisted up I was about her secret until she said those words. "But first... come home with me," I murmur against her lips.

She lifts a brow. "A sleepover sounds fun."

"Wasn't planning on sleeping."

I've never let myself believe I could have everything I wanted, but between her and my music, I'm so damned close.

## 16

_Annie_

I wake up to light streaming through the window.

I'm in Tyler's bed, wearing only his T-shirt.

I inch toward the side of it, but a tattooed arm bands around me.

"Come back," the arm's owner grunts.

Before I can respond, Tyler tugs me back against his warm, hard body.

Last night I went to see his show, and he was incredible. Then we came back to his apartment, where Tyler shut the door on Beck with barely a hello.

I would have protested if I hadn't wanted him so badly too.

After the amount of sex we've had, that wanting should've worn off.

It's unreal that it hasn't.

"I have morning breath," I warn as I turn in his arms.

"Don't care."

He pulls me against him, kissing me.

He tugs the hem of my T-shirt up and off, and I run my hands over his beautiful body.

"Again?" I tease lightly as I feel him harden between us.

"Uh-huh." His mouth drops to my breast, sucking marks into my skin, and I arch against him. "Not close to done."

My fingers thread into his hair, but I protest because it feels like the right thing to do and because I love how he responds. "But I'll see you at Leo's tonight. I'll come home with you after."

"Too late."

I squirm against him. "I have Entertainment Management in ninety minutes."

"Don't need it. You're dating a rock star."

I slap a hand against his shoulder, and he chuckles, his mouth vibrating on my skin. "Your hands aren't that good," I try.

"Really? You thought they were last night." His

fingers brush between my thighs where I'm already wet, and it's game over.

After reaching for a condom and rolling it on, he turns me on my side, slipping behind me and pressing between my legs.

"Good," I mumble. "I'm sick of your face too."

Tyler nips my neck in retaliation, and I hitch a breath.

He presses inside me, one inch at a time. I try to keep quiet because Beck's in the other room, but when Tyler's fingers find my clit, I can't hold back the moan.

"Knew you liked my hands," he murmurs in my ear. "What do you like best—my hands, my mouth, or my cock?"

I arch my ass into him, grinding because I need more even though he's already filling me everywhere. "I like your hands busy, your mouth quiet, and your cock in me."

"Good answer."

Then words are gone because he's chasing me into a wicked rhythm that drags us both to our peak way too soon and not soon enough.

After, I put on panties and the T-shirt so I can get up to use the bathroom. Tyler tugs on sleep pants, knotting them distractingly low around his hips, and follows me out.

Beck nods at us from the kitchen with a grin. "You want a third? I'm down to party."

I laugh, and Tyler shoots him side-eye.

It takes all of ten minutes to throw on my clothes and get ready to go.

"Don't walk home by yourself. Shower here, and we can go to school together," Tyler offers.

"I'm fine," I insist. "The neighborhood's not that bad, and I need to go to my room before class."

Beck holds out a bagel. "Parting gifts. Please come again."

I take it from him with a grin. "I'm sure I will."

With a last look at Tyler, who's watching me like he might drag me back to his room if I linger too long, I head outside and walk home.

The sunlight is amazing. Life is amazing.

Each block I travel lifts my spirits more.

As I'm finishing my bagel, my phone buzzes.

"Hi, Dad," I answer as I turn the corner, just able to catch a glimpse of the Vanier building a few blocks away. "I was actually just thinking about you. I need to send you something. It's an invitation, actually."

"Well, you can tell me about it in person. I had some business in New York and thought we could meet. Surprise."

I pull up fast enough someone bumps me from behind. "No way. You're... um... here now?"

"Yeah. I have a couple things to do this morning. Figured we could hang out after your classes."

"Great." My mind races, trying to piece together the truth and the lies. I press a hand to my suddenly damp forehead. "But let's meet somewhere. With midterms and all, I'm dying to get off campus."

When I get to the front doors of Vanier, I spot someone who has no business being here.

My stomach plummets as I pull up and my dad's gaze meets mine.

"What are you doing here?" I blurt.

There's no shock in his eyes.

"I want to know the same thing." Even as he tugs the baseball cap down on his head, he leaves the sunglasses off—which tells me he's really pissed if he's willing to risk being recognized.

I swallow, staring past him. "How did you find me?"

"An old industry contact thought he recognized

you at his studio. Then he saw your name on a lineup for a showcase and sent it to me."

*Fuck.* "Dad, I—"

"How long have you been planning this behind my back? And Haley's?"

I've heard my dad yell before, but this is different. His voice is low and precise and scary as fuck.

"It wasn't a plan. I auditioned in the spring," I admit.

His anger is a living thing, scorching the fall air between us. "I've asked you questions, Haley, too, about your classes, your residence—all of it. You lied to our faces."

Righteousness shoves out the guilt. "I told you I wanted to get more involved in music. I pitched you Vanier half a dozen times."

"I thought you were taking an interest. I thought you had priorities. Instead, my own daughter has been lying to me for months."

I drop my book bag on the pavement. Part of my brain insists I need to go to class, but I shove it aside. "You're acting as if people never lie. Everyone does. You do."

"About what?"

"You knew about me for a year and wouldn't acknowledge me."

His tight jaw goes slack, but it's the shock in his eyes I feel the most. I wasn't planning to tell him I knew that, not ever, but now that it's out, I can't take it back.

"I don't know what you're talking about." Dad's voice is unusually rough.

"I have a letter from my birth mom. She tried to contact me two years ago."

He exhales hard. "Annie, listen to me—you're my kid, and everything I've done was for you."

I shove both hands through my hair. "I get that you were the biggest star on the planet and you left because of me. Because you had a kid to take care of. I know you've made sacrifices"—I swallow—"but I'm eighteen. You can stop now."

His eyes, the same glowing gold as mine, deepen. "You want to be a grown-up? To face the world on your own without help from the people who care about you? Then I can stop sending tuition money. I assume this is where it's been going rather than Columbia." He gestures to the building behind me. "I should've been suspicious when you asked me to send money for tuition and your other expenses together and that you'd take care of getting everything paid. But you've always been a thoughtful kid and I trusted you. Hell, I was proud of you."

The blood drains from my face, guilt warring with devastation in my stomach.

Normally, I embrace every emotion I'm feeling. Today, they feel like weakness, and I need strength.

I know I'm in the wrong here, but he is too.

The Vanier building isn't only the backdrop of our argument. It's the reason I risked everything I am, everything I have.

I swallow down the emotions so I can find my voice. When I do, it's stronger than I expected.

"Do you have any idea how hard it is to get in here?"

He shakes his head. "That's not the point."

"Of course it's not. The point is you think I'm not good enough for this life. You never felt that way about Tyler."

Dad holds up a hand, gaze narrowing. "This isn't about Tyler. But it will be—"

"You tell yourself you want to protect me," I continue, raising my voice, "because when you were eighteen, you signed a deal with Wicked. You went on tour. You had *me*."

I'm losing ground in the battle with my emotions, and they're threatening to spill over.

"Just because you fucked up your life at eighteen doesn't mean I will." Tears burn down my face as I spin, grabbing my book bag and lunging for the doors. I pull up for a moment at the figure I see just outside them, looking between us with shock.

*Rae.*

I stalk past her, making my way through the halls. I skip the elevator to take the stairs two at a time. On my floor, I pass Elle's open door, where she's grabbing her books for class.

"Aren't you going to Entertainment Management?" she asks.

"No." I unlock my door and shove myself inside.

Footsteps sound behind me, but I don't look up. I grab the photo of me and my dad off my dresser and chuck it under my bed.

I drop onto my bed and press the heels of my hands to my eyes.

"Whoa. What happened?" Elle's voice is concerned.

I blink to see her and Rae hovering in the doorway. "Don't worry about it. You guys have class."

They exchange a look. "Fuck it. It was a boring topic lecture anyway," Rae says.

A grateful breath trembles out of my lips as she

takes a seat in her chair, Elle dropping onto my bed.

So, I tell them both everything, starting with my dad and how I auditioned and that I kept who I was a secret.

When I finish, Elle doesn't look pissed, she looks perplexed. "So, why'd you hide it?"

Rae answers for me. "Because in high school, people knew who she was, and they either hated her or wanted something from her."

"And you thought that'd follow you here," Elle interprets.

I nod.

"There's a problem with your logic," she replies. "High school's full of assholes."

My lips twitch despite my heavy heart.

Rae asks, "Why was he so sure he should've known you were here?"

"I don't know. He's never so much as mentioned Vanier in a conversation." But Rae's comment has me remembering something my dad said.

*"This isn't about Tyler. But it will be."*

He sounded angry, and not only with me.

But when Tyler left a year and a half ago, Dad

didn't give any indication they were still in touch. And this fall, Tyler would have told me.

*Right?*

"So, are we still going to Leo's tonight?" Elle prompts.

I suck in a breath, making a decision. "Yeah, we're going to Leo's."

---

# Tyler

My phone's on silent for most of the day, through my classes and guitar lesson. I leave it off while I'm messing with part of the song Annie and I are doing for the showcase.

When I unlock it back at home after grabbing a quick bite and showering to change for Leo's, I pull up in the middle of the living room.

The voicemail button shows a new message, and my phone shows three missed calls from the same number.

I hit play on the voicemail, my abs clenching even before Jax's voice barks from the speaker.

"Why is my daughter at Vanier, Tyler? And don't bother telling me you didn't notice. You sat at my table last week and acted like nothing was wrong."

Jax left me this voicemail this afternoon, which means...

*Annie.*

I try her number but don't get an answer.

So, I grab my coat and head for Leo's as quick as I can, turning over Jax's call on the way.

I get that he's pissed, but I'm pissed too. He didn't tell me she was struggling last year. He made me believe she was better off without me.

Jax might be my mentor, but I will always have Annie's back. Whatever she told him or didn't, that's their business, just like what's between her and me is ours.

I get to Leo's and use the back door to get inside. The place is already filling up, and as the act on stage finishes to applause, I crane my neck to look around the bar.

Impatience clashes with worry in my stomach until I spot her through the crowd. I press between bodies to reach her.

"Annie. Wait." I catch up to her near the stage doors. She's wearing dark jeans and a tank top, her hair down in waves around her head, but even in the darkness, I can tell her eyes are puffy.

I reach for her arms, but she steps back, her eyes filling with accusation. "My dad showed up today. He was pissed because he thought you should've told him I was at Vanier. Since you guys are so tight."

"Six," I say, careful. "I didn't tell him anything."

"So, you were in touch. How often? Once a week? Only on holidays?"

My hands fist at my sides. "I don't know... Every couple months?"

"While I was crying over you, you were talking to my dad as if nothing was wrong." Annie shakes her head, expression full of disbelief.

"It wasn't like that."

"Like what? Like you chose him over me? Because that's how it feels."

My gut twists, hard. She can't possibly see it like that. "I'm sorry for hurting you. I can't ever tell you how sorry. But I realized something this fall—we're not over." I step closer, and she angles her chin up to hold my gaze. I thread my fingers into her hair, cupping her neck in my hand.

"We're a song. You and me. What happened before was the first verse, and there's so much more."

Her fingers wrap around my wrist, but she doesn't try to move away. "Don't you ever wonder if maybe we're meant to be alone?" Her voice is stilted, and every muscle in me strains against the urge to crush her against me. "The liars, the rebels, the dreamers. Up there on the stage, in the spotlight, we bleed to make other people feel. But in order to bleed, we have to be broken."

It takes a moment for me to catch up to her words. "No. I don't think that." I jerk my chin toward the door. "Let's get out of here. Come back to my place. Or yours, I don't care. We'll talk."

Annie sucks in a breath. "I don't need to talk, Tyler."

The firmness of her voice hits me squarely in the chest. "I've wasted months—years—pretending I don't care about you," I insist. "I'm not doing it again."

Annie's eyes shine as she steps out of my hold, brushing her thumb across my palm before she drops my hand and moves closer.

"I care about you too. But my dad was right about one thing—it's easy to be shortsighted. This showcase is my first real chance. And it's your second, which matters even more."

"What are you saying?" The words feel hollow.

"That maybe we should take some room to breathe while we get through the showcase and focus on our dreams."

The clawing feeling in my chest wants to argue with her that we can do both, but the look on her face stops me.

It's not a goodbye, but it fucking feels like it. Anything but her coming home with me tonight is suddenly insufficient.

When Annie turns to head for the stage doors, my heart goes with her.

# 17

# Annie

"Have you talked to your dad?" Elle whispers from her spot next to me in the last row of pews.

I shake my head. "And the deposit that usually comes to my account isn't there."

Elle takes the Bible in the pew in front of her, fingering the pages. "That sucks."

We're at the funeral of a man I don't know—a banker, apparently, who loved fly fishing. No one seems particularly torn up he's gone except for a woman we passed on the way in who said she was his granddaughter. I gave her the entire stash of tissues from my bag, and the guilt I felt for being here was washed out by the gratitude on her face.

It's been nearly a week since my dad showed up in New York and I told Tyler I needed space.

Since then, we've rehearsed together three times at school, separately between that. I haven't been to his place, and he hasn't come to my room. He doesn't try to pressure me when we're together.

I'm grateful. I know deep down I can't blame Tyler for having a relationship with my dad, but I can't go there right now—not with the showcase looming. It's the biggest chance for both of us to grab what we've wanted for so long.

"It's fine," I tell my friend. "I'll get loans, and a job. I just wish everyone didn't suddenly know who I am and whisper in the halls. I thought Rae and I were getting along, but I don't know who else would've spread the word."

Elle huffs out a breath. "I asked him to take down the video."

I blink. "What video?"

The service concludes, and I grab Elle's sleeve, tug her after me down the row and out the door into the gray day.

My friend pulls up her phone, and I see an entry on Beck's vlog captioned: "Jax Jamieson's daughter crushing it," accompanied by a video of me performing at Leo's.

"Are you kidding me?"

I hit his contact on my phone.

"What's up, Manatee?" Beck drawls.

"You put me on your vlog?!"

I can hear the confusion in his voice. "Come on. People spotted your pop at Vanier this week. It's public knowledge now. Besides, I'm proud of you."

The backs of my eyes burn, but he continues. "What were you gonna do? Lie forever?"

"Maybe." I realize how dumb it sounds.

"I'm sorry, okay? I didn't think it'd be such a big deal. All we want in this place is to have someone notice us, and you have an excuse right there in your name and you don't use it."

"That's exactly why I don't," I insist. "Come on Beck—would you want that? If your dad was your ticket to being noticed, but he still disapproved of you, would you want that to be the very thing that makes your dreams come true?"

He turns it over. "No," he says at last. "It wouldn't be my dream anymore."

"Exactly."

The truth of it hangs between us for a moment before Beck speaks again. "I'll take it down."

"You know what? Don't worry about it."

It's too late to do much more damage, and some part of his words are right—I can't hide who I am forever.

I'm going to have to be this much more committed to being noticed on my own terms.

"Listen," Beck starts again, "I don't know what's happening with you and Ty, but Zeke put our boy on ice."

That has me paying attention.

"He promised Tyler a meeting after he slayed that show last week. But it was mysteriously canceled two days later and not rescheduled. Zero explanation."

*Shit.* Tyler never mentioned it.

I'd never stopped to think about what my dad would do to Tyler. If my dad pulled his support or said something to Zeke to make him doubt Tyler...

"The showcase will fix it," I say, half to myself and half to Beck. "He'll crush it, and someone smarter than Zeke will recognize how talented he is and give him a chance."

"You think so, Manatee? They might be more interested in Jax Jamieson's kid."

It's the validation I wanted but for the wrong reasons, and the cost...

I hate that it could cost Tyler his chance.

I hang up and find Elle behind me, arms folded. I relay what Beck told me.

"So, your dad can say one word and Tyler's shot is gone," Elle comments.

The unfairness of it has resolve hardening in my gut. "No," I decide. "He can't."

---

The morning of the showcase, I wake up to a text.

**Tyler: Hey, I was thinking about you last night. Not about you in my bed, though I swear I can still smell you on my pillows, and I hate the thought that it might fade before you're back, but about how you look when we're practicing. How strong you are. How much I believe in you. Whether today's the start of something or the end, there's no one I'd rather be up there with.**

I get out of bed and stumble to the bathroom. I take a hot shower and wash my hair, letting the heat scald every inch of me.

It's not until I'm halfway through drying my hair that I realize what I have to do.

I send a text back to Tyler.

**Annie: I can't do the showcase.**

My phone rings while I'm pulling on jeans.

"What happened?" Tyler's voice is full of disbelief and concern.

I take a steadying breath. "With everything going on with my dad, I just can't. I'm sorry, Tyler. You have to do our song yourself. You can sing it and play it. You know it inside out."

There's a pause before he replies, "We need to talk about this."

"We don't. You'll do great."

"Annie—"

I click off, squeezing the phone in my hand hard enough it leaves marks in my palm.

The fall showcase is attended by a few thousand people. Each seat is filled by someone from industry, all of them eagerly anticipating the new crop of talent, hoping to discover the flame that will take their career to the next level.

That afternoon, I stand at the back of the auditorium, out of sight, and watch the first half dozen performers. I'm the only one here, which is why I'm lingering by the back doors.

Also, I can make a quick escape if I need to.

"What are you doing here? I thought you were performing."

Pen's incredulous voice has me sagging against the wall. She folds me in a hug while I explain.

The disbelief and sorrow on her face are everything I'm feeling.

"A, this was everything you wanted."

"I thought it was," I admit. "But I couldn't stand the thought of him not getting what he wanted when it was my fault. When I could help him."

As if he hears my thoughts, Tyler appears on stage. From the distance, I search his face and body for signs he's lain awake this week as much as I have. I study his broad shoulders, his easy grace as he takes the microphone.

Tyler scans the audience as if he's looking for someone. My chest contracts more.

*I'm here. I've got you.*

When he plays, his fingers rest heavier than usual on the strings. Each chord reverberates through my soul. But when his low voice joins overtop, my heart stops altogether.

In that moment, I realize a truth, one I hate as much as I love...

Tyler's not broken. He's beautiful.

There's a crackling in the audience, a kinetic energy. Emotions chase each other through my chest. My fingers find the rose under the neckline of my shirt, and I squeeze it hard enough the edge bites into my palm.

My prince is playing our song, and from the first words, it's not our song anymore—it's his.

From the first chorus, he's not mine anymore.

He's theirs.

I don't know if I envy him or the audience. Both, I think, everyone part of that experience I'm suddenly outside of.

Tears sting the backs of my eyes.

Something bumps my hip, and I glance over to see my friend. "Let's get out of here for the weekend," Pen murmurs. "You and me."

My chest thaws a few degrees. "I love you. But given my dad put a stop on next semester's tuition, that's probably not the best idea."

"Pssh. I went to Columbia like my parents wanted. I'm flush. You pick a place, anywhere you want." She gives me another squeeze. "Think about it. I have to go pee."

I show her to the bathroom up one level, which is quiet even during performances.

Everyone's at the showcase, and the only sound up here comes from the open door of a rehearsal room.

My feet carry me there, and I lean in.

"Why aren't you at the showcase?" I ask Finn.

He glances up from the piano. "Why aren't *you* at the showcase? Figured Jax Jamieson might come."

I step into the room and lean my elbows on the ebony wood. "So, you heard."

Finn lets out a low chuckle. "I don't care what your name is. I'm thinking about the three shows I'm doing in LA in the next week. I need to get out of New York. It's too cold, the weather and the people."

"Hey, Finn," I say, feeling impulsive, and he cocks his head. "You made me an offer the night I sang with you to get me tickets to your shows in LA."

"Still stands."

"Thank you. But it's not tickets I want."

## 18

# Tyler

"Annie. Open up." I pound on the door at the end of the hall on the sixth floor.

The third time I knock, it swings wide to reveal Rae. "She's not here, lover boy."

"Do you know when she's getting back?"

She shrugs, glancing over her shoulder. "Few days, I think. She asked me to feed Heath."

The goldfish circles his tank as if everything's right with the world.

*It's not right.*

I shove both hands through my hair. "I've been calling her all day since the showcase."

"Bet it's hard. Sounds like your phone's the one blowing up."

She's not wrong. The thing jumps in my pocket every damned minute.

The performance was good—better than good.

But it wasn't *right*... because she wasn't with me.

I head back to my place, my breath huffing in the November air, and find a new slew of texts and voicemails.

One missed call from Annie has me relieved because it means she's not avoiding me.

This time, I get through. "I've been calling all night," I say when she picks up.

"Sorry, it's been kind of crazy. I wanted to tell you how great you were."

I tune in to the background noise, realize she's keeping her voice down.

"I watched from the back," she goes on. "Like you watched *The Little Mermaid*."

My throat works. "Best seats in the house."

"They are if you're on your way out of town."

I exhale hard. "You're going home to talk to your dad and Haley. That's good, Annie. It'll be good."

"No. I'm going to LA with Pen. I'm going to play a few gigs with Finn."

Her words have me pulling up in the middle

of an intersection, which I don't realize until a horn honks at me and I force myself to keep walking.

"You bailed on our performance, but you're playing gigs in LA with Finn?" Anger seeps into my tone even though I don't know what I'm pissed about.

Maybe that we put all this work in, that I did this for her, and she walked away like it didn't matter.

"It's not like that, Tyler." I wish she was here so I could look her in the damned eyes, so I could grab her arms and tell her not to leave. "It's something I need to do for myself. You were really great. I'm so proud of you."

She clicks off before I can argue.

The street signs say I'm halfway between Vanier and my apartment, yet somehow I'm utterly lost.

I've never stalked someone on social media before, but there's a first time for everything.

All day Saturday, I'm scanning Annie's feeds. She doesn't post often and is careful when she does, so it's not surprising I come up empty, but Sunday morning, I switch to a new strategy.

"Look at you, creeper."

I look up from the kitchen table as my roommate comes in the front door.

"You can't tell I'm a creeper from ten feet away."

"It's called a logical inference. You were creeping when I left; ergo, you're more than likely creeping still."

I glare at my roommate, holding up the phone. "There's a picture of him on stage, the fucking prick. And she's next to him."

He crosses to me, narrowing his gaze on the screen. "Ah. It took you a day to switch to the best friend's feed? Rookie."

Annie's not tagged, but I see her, and I want to throw the phone across the room.

Beck pulls a stack of mail out of his jacket pocket and passes me an envelope. "This came for you. I had to sign for it and everything."

Halfheartedly, I open it and glance inside. "A check for ten thousand dollars from the showcase."

I glance at Beck's lighter on the counter.

"You are not burning that check," Beck drawls

as he shrugs out of his coat and hangs it by the door. "You earned it. You lit that auditorium up, and no one who witnessed it could deny that fact."

I tug on my hair. "I don't know why she'd work so hard for this, then bail. She wanted it. It was her moment too, her fucking song."

He drops into the chair across from me. "You really have no clue why she'd put you on that stage alone."

I straighten, not liking the sound of those words. "No. Tell me."

A guilty expression crosses his face. "I told her Zeke pulled your meeting. She knew you lost your shot because of her and Jax and if she did the showcase, you might lose that too. She didn't screw you, Ty. She saved you."

Emotions collide inside me—disbelief and frustration and longing.

My head falls back on a groan. "Dammit, Beck!"

I shove out of my seat and grab my phone, hurling it across the room so it slams into the living room wall.

I whirl to face him, staring him down as if this is his fault. "She wanted space, and I let her have it." I stalk across the room, intending to grab the phone, but when I get there, I take a pillow off the couch and hurl it toward the kitchen instead.

"How does she do this?!" I shout.

Beck eyes me as if he's watching some strange creature never before discovered by humans as I continue to rant.

"She's always a mess of feelings. She can take it, but me? I can't hold it in, wall it up, or shove it down." I scan the room, feeling more than a little unhinged.

But I know I could throw everything in this entire apartment and it wouldn't be enough.

"Fuck this. I'm going after her," I decide. "I won't be the guy who left her again."

I start toward the front door, but Beck grabs my shirt.

"You're not the guy who left her," he says as I stop angrily next to him. "You're the guy who's giving her what she asked for."

"You want me to sit here like an asshole."

"Or you could deal with your damned emotions like everyone else." He holds up a finger, telling me not to move.

I exhale hard as he goes to my room, comes back with the guitar Annie bought me. Twenty-four frets. Rosewood. Made to fit in my hands.

I take the neck in my hands, turn it over.

It's mine. Today, maybe it's the only thing that is.

I carry the guitar to the kitchen table and drop onto my seat. I don't know what I want to play, but my fingers do until one song slips into the next.

*In the spotlight, we need to bleed. We need to be broken.*

Eventually, the emotions rise to the surface, one chasing the next until I'm bent over the guitar.

I'm playing and singing and who the hell knows what else, but I'm pouring all of me out, everything I can't contain.

When I lift my head, I see Beck's intent expression trained on me, along with the camera of his phone.

I don't care.

I do the only thing I can.

I play until my fingers are raw.

19
———

# *Annie*

"So, then he moons the cops and runs ten blocks with his pants around his knees," Pen says, clanking her glass on the side table in the dressing room for emphasis.

"And this guy's running for treasurer?" I reply.

"Apparently."

We're backstage after Finn's second show in LA. The past two days have been nuts between rehearsals and soundchecks and hanging out with my friend.

It feels strange not doing my own material after all my work for the showcase.

But I'm working—as a singer. Finn's people not only paid for the hotel—I'm actually getting compensated.

"Annie! That's Annie Jamieson. Jax Jamieson's kid." I turn to see the guys bent over the coffee table, and Finn waves me over.

"You must've grown up backstage," one of the guys drawls. "Bet you have some great stories."

I cross to them, the cowboy boots I changed into after the show clacking on the hard floor. "Honestly, I was a kid the last time he toured. And the best stories I have of him are personal."

I haven't talked to my dad since coming to LA. Haley called me last night, but it was a short conversation. I can tell she's disappointed, which hurts too, but she said she'd work on him as far as tuition. Clearly, she doesn't agree with his position, but I don't see her going behind his back unless I really need something.

"We'll take personal stories," Finn says with a grin, slinging an arm over the back of the couch.

My dad's name is currency here. It gives me renewed appreciation for the way Tyler was always chill about it.

*More than that, he lied for me.*

I shove the thought away.

"You know what?" I ask. "You should be remembering nights like tonight instead of asking for old stories. Someday you won't be asking me about him. You'll be asking him about *me*." I arch a brow, and a round of hollers goes up.

I cut a look back at Pen, and she nods. "We're gonna get out of here. Thanks for the gig," I tell Finn, starting for the door.

Pen goes to grab her things while Finn follows me toward the hall. "Don't take it personally. Someday you'll have stories. Until then, the sexiest thing about you is him."

I size him up. "Did you know who my dad was when you took me on? Before it came out at school?"

He grins. "I did my homework. Can't fault me for that."

Some of the joy I felt about making it to LA on my own merit falls away, but I refuse to let it vanish entirely.

Beck's right. I'll always be Jax Jamieson's kid, and I need to make peace with that.

Even if my dad and I can't find a way to make peace with each other.

Pen joins me, and I nod to Finn. "I'll see you tomorrow for the final show."

I grab my friend, and we take off back to our hotel.

"I'm glad you came with me this weekend. It means a lot," I say.

"Of course! I can afford to make a DIY long weekend by blowing off a single day of classes."

November in LA is balmy as hell. I stick my hands in the pockets of my jean shorts as we pass palm trees.

"I've been wondering if I made the right call in going to Vanier instead of Columbia. The highs and the lows are a kind of extreme I've never experienced, not even when I learned Jax was my dad or when Carly tortured me."

"Well, if you ever decided to transfer to Columbia, obviously I'd be supportive," Pen says. "We'd have a fabulous apartment with a wine fridge, and I'd be the best sommelier-slash-roommate ever."

My chest expands. "I'll miss you when you go back tomorrow. And I'm taking you to the airport whether you like it or not."

"You'll spend the whole day in traffic," she warns. "You should just fly back with me."

I kick a stone on the pavement with my boot, thinking about everything that's gone down.

"Nah, I'll stay and do the final show tomorrow

night. But I do want to see Elle and Beck. Hell, maybe even Rae."

"And Tyler."

"Definitely Tyler."

His handsome face appears in my mind. I wish I had him to talk to. I know what I'd say.

*I miss you.*

*I shouldn't have blamed you.*

*I'm sorry I fucked up your chance in this industry.*

Back in the hotel, Pen's sprawled across the other double bed when my phone buzzes on my nightstand.

**Elle: You need to see this.**

It's a link for Beck's vlog. Something's glitchy though, because the number of followers is off by a few zeroes.

I reload the page, but it shows the same thing. It's not only the follower count that's off—it's the views.

The top video is one called "Unhinged." Most of Beck's videos are ten or fifteen minutes, but this one's nearly an hour long.

I hit Play.

It's Tyler sitting on his bed with his guitar. My

heart sticks in my throat. A few seconds in, I hear Tyler's voice, humming over the chords.

He's riveting. From the comments, a lot of people think so—hundreds of thousands of likes, more than one million views.

"Shit. Is that him?" Pen drops onto the bed next to me. I didn't know she was still awake.

I turn up the volume. Then Tyler sings, and I recognize the words.

Because they're mine.

The words are from our showcase song at first, then another and another.

Comments from people saying he's talented, he's gorgeous, and I stop reading the comments because they're meaningless. The only thing that matters is him.

"Pen, I'm in love with Tyler."

The words hang between us. The only backdrop is the music continuing to stream from my phone.

"Well, obvs."

My chin snaps up as I seek out her gaze in the dark. "What should I...?" I shove a hand through my hair. "I need to tell him."

"That might be a good start," she says with a half smile.

I pause the video and open a text window, typing a message to Beck with shaking hands.

**Annie: Your vlog exploded. What's going on?!**

Then I pull up a browser window.

"I need to look for flights," I say under my breath. "Maybe I can get on yours."

Finding a Monday flight on Sunday night is hit or miss, but there are a few options since it's a popular route. But before I can book anything, my phone buzzes with an incoming call.

"Beck," I say breathlessly.

"Hey. Ty had a meeting with Zeke today."

"On the weekend?"

"Guess they saw the video and decided they couldn't wait. They put a contract in front of him and everything."

Emotions wash over me. There's pride, overwhelm, happiness. "That's... wow."

Pen shakes her head, eyes wide. *What?* she mouths.

I hold up a finger as Beck continues. "Yeah. I'm sure he'll want to tell you himself."

"I can't wait."

"But... don't hurry back to New York, all right?" Beck says, and it sounds like a warning.

What's going on? Is Tyler doing better without me? Did he say something to Beck about wanting space, too?

I swallow the disappointment that rises up. "Okay. Can you tell him... tell him I'm so happy for him. And if he wants to talk, I'm here."

"Ah. Sure. It's early here, Manatee. I gotta get ready for class."

I swallow as I hang up, reminding myself to be thrilled. Tyler's getting everything he ever wanted, and that's enough.

---

The next day, I take Pen to the airport and hug her for ages. "Text me when you get home, okay?" I say when I pull back. "Thank you for everything."

"No prob. I needed a few days of sunshine and drama after midterms anyway."

When I get back to the hotel, I spend the afternoon swimming and working on some homework, trying not to check my phone to see if Tyler's called.

But there's nothing.

Not before I head to the venue to get ready for the gig.

Not after.

Not when I get back and order delivery from a restaurant down the street before I take a hot shower and steam the makeup off my face.

"Well," I say in the silent bathroom. "Here we are."

I booked a flight back tomorrow after the final show using my credit card, which I'll have to pay for—and I will.

Skipping the showcase was a setback, but it's not the end. I'm more determined than ever to succeed.

I'll get a job. I'll see if there's anything part-time at Vanier or maybe the library at Columbia. I haven't waited tables, but I could do that, too. I'll do anything. I'll learn to stand on my own feet.

I pull on clean underwear, then reach for the sleep T-shirt on the counter and tug it over my head.

Staring at my reflection, I suddenly remember wearing the Ramones T-shirt the night after Tyler saved me at the cast party.

Now, I'm grown-up enough to save myself. I'm also grown-up enough to know that what I feel for

Tyler isn't some passing thing—I love him. I miss him. I crave his company. In the silent hotel room, a wave of longing hits me.

The knock on the door makes my stomach growl.

I switch off the bathroom light and cross the hotel room.

When I answer the door, every thought evaporates.

A gorgeous guy with a day's scruff blocks the light from the hallway. In a bomber jacket and faded jeans, his hair falls across his face as if he's been running his hands through it all night.

"Hi, Six."

20

Tyler

When Annie opens the door of her hotel room, her face slackens in shock.

But what I notice most is how damned beautiful she looks in her gray oversized T-shirt, her hair falling in wet curls around her shoulders. Her face is bare, her lips full and enticing as she takes me in.

"You're not the delivery guy," she murmurs.

"You were going to open the door looking like that?"

My gaze drags down her body, the way her damp hair leaves wet spots on her shirt, dripping down across her breasts. Her legs are miles long under the hem, begging a man to sell his soul for the chance to wrap them around his waist.

Her lips curve. "I was really hungry."

She moves to let me in, and I follow, the door clicking shut behind me.

"I saw your video on Beck's vlog," she says as I take in the modest but tidy room with two double beds. "You were amazing."

"Thanks." Her praise warms me in a way no one else's can.

"Do you want to sit?" she gestures around us, but the only place is the bed. I shake my head. It's safer to talk like this, standing up, a few feet between us.

"Nah. I've been sitting on a plane all day."

She nods, weaving her hands together in front of her. "What are you doing here? Beck told me you took a meeting with Zeke and he offered to sign you again. Congratulations."

"I didn't sign."

Annie lifts her chin, eyes widening in surprise. "Why not?"

*Because you're my business. More so than any agents or producers.*

I want to close all the distance between us but settle for half of it.

"I was sitting in the chair across from him and thinking about what happened the last time I signed, and I realized something."

I take a slow breath, not missing the significance of this moment, of what I'm about to say—of what I can't keep inside any longer.

"I didn't go off the rails because of my dad or the contract or New York. It was because I was finally starting to believe in my dreams and you weren't there for it."

Annie's eyes shine, and I force myself to keep going because I have to get through what I came here to say, and if she breaks down, it's gonna be even harder.

"I know you think I chose Jax over you. But I chose you a long time ago. Over everything and everyone. And you chose me."

I shove both hands through my hair, the emotions rising up.

"When you gave me that guitar in high school, you gave me you. I was too young and stupid to understand that. I was convinced our feelings would fuck up your life or mine. But twice I've had that moment where my dreams are about to come true, and twice it's been meaningless without you.

And I know I'm stubborn, but I won't make the same mistake."

The distance between us is unbearable, so I close it, wrapping my hands around her bare arms under the T-shirt sleeves. "I see you, Annie. I've always seen you. At your best, your worst, everything in between. And even when you fuck things up, I want a front-row seat because it's so damn beautiful." My voice cracks. "I love you, Six. You're the only song I wanna sing, the only movie I wanna watch, the only"—now I'm grasping—"food I wanna eat."

Annie sucks in a trembling breath as her gaze searches my face as if she's looking for evidence of my words.

She'll find it. On every inch of me, she'll find it.

"Beck told me what you did by stepping back from the showcase for me," I continue, needing to finish. "I wish you hadn't, and I would have tried to stop you if I'd known, but I can't seem to stop you from doing anything. It's maddening, and it's one more thing I love about you.""

I brush a thumb across her lower lip because the pull between us it too strong to resist. She doesn't try to stop me, and the softness of her skin, coupled with the way she lets me touch her, has conviction and possessiveness rising up.

"Now it's my turn to do something you don't want. You asked me for space, and I tried to give it to you. But I won't let you push me away because you think anything, anyone, matters more to me than you. You'll always be wrong."

We're standing flush, her chest brushing mine in a way that reminds me she's practically naked.

Her expression's colored with caring and something more than that, something bold and edgy, and it tugs at me.

"You want to eat me?" she asks softly.

I slide my fingers into her damp hair, cupping her face. "That's what you took from my speech?"

She bites her lip, and my thumb strokes up her soft jaw in a way that makes her eyes darken.

"I love you too, Tyler."

*Holy fuck.*

My chest expands until it's near breaking. Her throat works, her hands wrapping around my wrists. But instead of pulling me away, she just holds them. Her dark lashes flutter as her attention drops to my mouth.

I never expected hearing those words would hit me so hard, but it does.

Maybe I've been waiting to hear them for longer than I thought.

"That's it?" I whisper even though I'm shaking, adoration blurring with the desire her touch stirs in me. "No poems, no songs, no anything?"

She shakes her head. "We don't need them."

She's right.

But there is something we do need, something that has my abs clenching, my entire body aware of every inch of hers.

"Tell me again," I mutter.

"I love you." Annie's response is instant, her gaze searching as if the answer I gave her is only part of what she's looking for.

She's mine—her heart, her soul, her body. I know it, but I want to prove it, want to show her I'm hers every bit as much.

My mouth claims hers, possessive and needy at once. She shifts up on her toes, wraps her arms around my neck, and crushes herself against me. Her body heat through the dampness of her T-shirt turns the fire inside me into a blaze.

She's as hungry as I am, teasing my tongue with hers, dragging her nails across my scalp in a way that has me groaning.

I lift her in my arms and carry her to the bed,

dropping her on the covers. In an instant, she's on her knees to meet me, reaching for my clothes.

I'm already hard for her. On a growl, I catch the backs of her thighs so she falls back on the mattress, and I follow her down.

My mouth drops to her waist, and I lift the hem of her shirt, pressing kisses against her hip at the edge of her panties.

I kiss my way up her ribcage. When I can't go any farther, I grasp the hem of her shirt and tug it over her head.

I take in every inch of flushed skin. I'm going to memorize the scent of her, the taste. I'm going to touch her until it's what she expects, until every second I'm not touching her, she's looking for me.

When I drop my mouth to her breast and suck, the way she fucking bows against my mouth says I'm on the right path.

I tease her for as long as we both can take it. Her hands are in my hair, dragging me closer, a demanding contrast to her soft floral scent and warm skin.

She's sweet and greedy, vulnerable and unconquerable.

I'm going to fuck this girl until she's ruined for anyone else.

My fingers slip between her legs, rubbing the panel of her panties.

It's soaked.

"Oh shit, Tyler."

My mouth is at her ear, my body flush with hers so I can absorb every shiver, every shudder, every muscle straining to get closer. "Say it again."

"Tyler."

I shove two fingers under her panties and press them inside her heat.

Annie's head falls back on the pillow, her damp hair fanned across the white sheets. She's my mermaid, my siren, the woman whose call I'll answer when I'm dead.

"I see you, Six," I mutter as I stroke her, finding that spot inside that makes her gasp. "I don't care where you're going as long as I go with you."

When I rub a circle over her clit, she says my name as if she's trying to finish a marathon and I'm the only hope of getting her through. Her nails dig into my biceps hard enough to leave marks.

Her touch grazes my abs above my jeans, her gaze meeting mine from under her half-lowered lashes.

The sound of my zipper and the brush of her fingers against my cock through my boxer briefs is a warning. She's writhing and panting with every stroke, and when she wraps her hand around my cock, I swear she gets wetter.

My abs clench, and I'm leaking all over her. I want her hands, her lips, her pussy—all of it, a never-ending carousel until we're both dizzy and spent.

But there's something I need first.

Her breath is a shallow pant, and my teeth find her earlobe, tugging hard enough she shakes.

"Come for me."

I growl the words, and she responds, her body bowing up, her hips grinding and squeezing on my fingers.

Forget music. Her orgasm is the most gorgeous thing I've ever experienced.

She comes down, and I stand up off the bed, stripping out of my clothes before getting a condom from my wallet.

I start to roll it on, but she reaches for my wrist. "I'm on the pill."

Her mouth sets in a firm line as the seriousness of this slams into me.

I've thought about how it would feel to have nothing between us but only in a fantasy kind of way, like I've thought about fucking her in her pool in Dallas, her skin slippery from the water, or on top of the piano in a rehearsal room at Vanier, her legs spread so wide I can see six octaves between her calves.

My chest tightens. "I've never gone without."

Her hands cup my face. "We don't have to. But I'd like to, if you would."

"Why?" The word is hoarse, barely audible.

A breath trembles out of her lips, but she continues. "Because I love you and I want to be so close to you it's impossible to tell where you end and I start. Because I want you to come inside me, for you to know that some part of you is in me… even though I know you always have been."

If she was planning to say something else, I'll never know because I cut her off.

I claim her lips with mine because I have to kiss her when she talks like that.

I'm a thousand feet tall—and harder than I can remember being—when I position myself against her entrance, where she's so wet from my touch, every easy slide of my cock on her skin a filthy promise of what's to come.

*Right there with you, Six.*

I memorize how she looks, feels, sounds, smells. Her fingers dig into my ass as I lower over her, our lips brushing. "You know something?" I murmur. "You're the only person who's ever made me want to believe."

Her voice is rough at the edges. "You're the only person I've never stopped believing in."

Those words break me.

I slide home, swallowing her cry as she takes every inch of me.

She feels so good—better than I dreamed.

This girl is everything. My past, my future. The home I never knew.

I'll bury myself so deep she'll never get me out.

I nudge us into a rhythm, but her body's greedy, barely letting me pull back so I can give us both the pleasure of stroking back in.

We're a tangle of need and feelings and sweat and hope. I'm torn between the need to draw this out for fucking hours and the drive to see how many times I can claim her before we leave this bed.

When my hand slides between us to find her clit, she gasps, eyes flying wide.

I draw nearly out of her, darkly thrilled by her moan of protest.

When I speak, my voice is a rasp.

"I..."

I press back inside on a long stroke, only to pull out.

"Dream."

Again.

"Of."

Again.

"*This*."

Annie comes, and the feeling of her gripping me drags me there too. She shakes in my arms, and I hold her tight, knowing nothing in life has ever felt this good... and for the first time, believing it's possible to keep feeling this way.

**21**

———

# *Annie*

Sex can't change a person. I get that intellectually.

But as I lie next to Tyler in the hotel bed, I want to argue with that statement.

A smile tugs across my face, and it's reflected in Tyler's expression as he shifts over me. "Hi," he murmurs.

"Hi."

His body's beautiful, strong, and muscled. As I trace the lines of his bare shoulders, his pec, his bicep, the ink has me staring again.

"Your food get lost on the way?" he asks.

I glance past him at the door, thinking for the first time in a long time about my meal. "Maybe they heard the noises and turned back."

Tyler presses his smiling mouth to my shoulder, and I grin too.

My fingers dig into his arms, holding him still as my attention drags back to the ink on his chest. "I can't believe you've had all these done since you left. Tell me about them?"

"Pick one and I will."

I bite my lip. "The boat and the waves."

"I got it after I left Dallas and spent the week at my dad's bedside. I remember feeling as if I was being tossed about in the storm. One night, all I could think was, 'I can't control the storm. I need a bigger boat'."

I trace the lines of the ship. "So, you got one."

"I can't control the world, but I can control myself. That there are things life can never take from me."

"Maybe you should write the songs," I murmur. "That's kind of beautiful. How do you come out with that?"

He leans down on both elbows, caging me in. "How do you write the lyrics you write?"

I wet my lips under his heavy stare. "Easy. When the boy you love leaves, there's an infinite supply of heartache to go around."

Pain flashes in his eyes. "Never again." He

lowers his lips to my jaw, and I thread my fingers into his hair. "But don't diminish yourself. You might've written when I left, but I'm not the reason. You have a talent that goes beyond the words. It's how you see the world."

I smile. "I love writing. Maybe even more than being on stage." It's the first time I've said it out loud.

Tyler doesn't look at me as if I'm nuts. In fact, he doesn't look surprised. "If that's what you want, I'm all in."

Warmth washes over me. "Can we stay here forever?" I take in the mountain of plush hotel blankets. "We could build a fort."

He skims lower, to my breast, and my laugh is cut off. "Go nuts, baby. I'll be right there."

God, he's good at touching me. Was he always this good, even without the practice? Or is it me— that I've wanted him so bad for so long that even the slightest reward has me going off? My body is a shimmer of sensation, the pleasure from his hands tracing a leisurely path down my sides to my hips blending with the lingering high from the orgasms.

When his hot mouth closes over my nipple, the sharp tug of need makes me moan. Judging from the way his hands get impatient and one slips between my thighs again, teasing me where I'm still wet from him, he likes that too.

There's a knock on the door.

Tyler ignores it, until it comes again.

"My food," I mumble.

With a groan and a blanket around his waist, Tyler goes to answer it. A moment later he comes inside, setting a paper bag on the desk.

He peers inside before cutting me a look, one brow lifted. "You ordered cheese fries without me."

I laugh. "Clearly, I knew you'd be coming."

Before I can tell him to forget the food, that I need him back here with me, Tyler's phone rings.

He rubs a hand over his face before hitting a button. "Hey, man."

"Did she leave?" Beck demands over the speaker.

I'm already missing Tyler's body heat, but when he cocks his head, grinning at me, I can forgive him. "She didn't leave. She's here."

"Hi, Beck," I call, shifting off the bed naked and crossing to grab one of the cheese fries off the desk before it gets cold.

Fucking yum.

"Hey, Manatee. Listen, Ty, your studio boys

want an answer. They've been buzzing at the door all day."

"They've been blowing up my phone, too." Tyler paces the length of the room, phone in one hand, rubbing the other through his hair until it sticks straight up.

God, he's beautiful. I still can't believe he didn't want to sign before talking to me.

I cross to him. My hand slides around his neck, feathering the hair at his nape, and he stops. He doesn't move, just lets me touch him as he watches me with pure and simple love.

"They sent one of those edible arrangements with fruit and chocolate and shit to the apartment," comes Beck's disembodied voice through the phone, reminding me he's still with us. "Not just the crappy cantaloupe, but strawberries and pineapple—"

"Thanks, Beck," Tyler says, his gaze locked on mine. "We'll catch a flight back tonight, so we'll be back in the morning."

"You guys really need to—"

Tyler clicks off and tosses the phone past me without looking.

I ask, "Are you going to take that offer?"

"What do you think I should do?" His hands

find my sides, skimming slowly down my hips in a way that makes me suck in a breath.

"I think you should read it. With a lawyer—"

"You're cold."

I frown. "Tyler, that's what they do for a living. I'm surprised you haven't—oh." I follow his gaze down to my pebbled nipples.

"Keep talking." He pulls my hips against his, where he's already getting hard again. His length is pinned between us, but the glimpses of his cock have me swallowing.

"Um... do you have a copy of the contract with you?"

Tyler backs me against the wall, grinding himself between my thighs as his mouth finds mine. "Uh-huh," he mutters between kisses.

His fingers stroke down my stomach, up the inside of my thighs.

I suck in a breath and try to concentrate. "There are probably some clauses to look out for."

I remember overhearing Haley and my dad talk about one of his contracts, but the moment Tyler's fingers slick across my skin and dip inside me, I can't for the life of me remember the details.

"Good." He sinks to his knees, nudging my legs

wider while he lifts his gorgeous face to meet my gaze.

*Holy hell.*

"What are you doing?" I pant.

"While you're making sure they don't fuck me, I'm gonna fuck you."

---

Tyler and I catch a red-eye back to New York. We spring for in-flight internet and look up lawyers on the way, and by the time we land, he has a meeting with a Midtown entertainment attorney to review Zeke's deal.

Tyler insists our car drop me off first and walks me to the doors at Vanier. "Have fun today."

"Thanks." With the flight and transport from the airport, I missed Entertainment Management and Talbot's class. The first isn't a big deal, but I'm going to apologize in person for the latter. "Good luck meeting Zeke."

Tyler kisses me long and hard before pulling back, brushing his thumb across my jaw.

I watch him go, biting my lip as he slides into the car. Is it ever going to sink in that he's mine? I hope not.

I take my bags upstairs, but no one's there—probably because it's still the middle of the day.

Sure enough, the dining hall's half-full with the pre-lunch coffee crowd when I pass on my way to the classrooms.

I linger by the door of Talbot's class until it lets out.

"Hey, traveler," Elle chirps when she sees me.

I grab her in a hug. "It's really good to see you."

"You too. Did you hug Rae like this? I'd pay to see that."

I pull back, smiling. "Haven't seen her yet. Just dropped my bags off."

"Miss Jamieson."

My good mood fades a little as I look over Elle's shoulder at Talbot.

"I'm sorry I missed class. I—"

"Please come see me at my office in thirty minutes."

"Um. Okay." I hadn't expected it to warrant an entire meeting, but I nod as she passes us, books in hand.

"That sounds ominous," Elle says.

"Right?"

"You missed a crazy few days," she continues as we start down the hallway. "All hell broke loose after the showcase. A few people got approached by agents, but the shit with Tyler was the craziest. Beck told me their entire apartment is full of gifts from people who want to meet Tyler."

"That is crazy."

"You guys good?"

I grin. "Yeah, actually. We are."

When I head to the central administration on the third floor, the admin assistant offers me a chair while I wait, and I wave her off with a smile, perusing the full-color photos on the wall. All are of people on stage: musicians, dancers, actors. There's grace in what they do, and competence, and triumph.

None of the blood and sweat and tears are in these photos. I know the personal toll it takes. We've lost students this year who've dropped out. I've seen the dancers with their bleeding feet weep when they sustain an injury, when normal people would be grateful for the reprieve from constant torture. Actors get contorted into so many roles and forms they don't know where they end and their characters begin. And the musicians...

Well, we spend our days and nights chasing something fleeting. The perfect song or verse or moment of connection with an audience—one that will be gone the moment it happens, unless like Beck with Tyler, someone managed to capture it.

We bend over backward to create something extraordinary.

None of us fit in, so we trade our souls, our bodies, our egos, our emotions, for a chance to stand out.

"Miss Jamieson."

The admin assistant motions me into Talbot's office, and I follow her, gathering myself and smoothing down my outfit. Talbot looks impassively at me as I take a seat across from her.

The door clicks quietly closed before she speaks. "Do you know why you're here?"

"I assume it's about missing class today. I'm sorry. I had a chance to perform with Finn—Mr. Harvey—in LA. I promise I won't miss any more classes this semester."

She rounds the desk to take her seat, folding her lined hands in her lap and levelling me with cool eyes. "And what about the showcase? What's your excuse for missing that?"

"That was... a bold choice," I concede.

"You turned your back on an opportunity every student waits their entire life for."

"I did it for someone I care about. And I'd do it again."

"Why?"

"When I came to Vanier, I wanted to prove myself, and I thought that meant getting attention at all costs. But some things matter more than the spotlight."

Her brows twitch, but I continue. "Since coming here, I've learned there's a lot more than a bunch of talented people who want to be famous. Everyone has their own reason for being here"—I think of Tyler, of Beck and Elle and Rae—"but we all want to connect to something. To be part of something bigger than us."

I shift forward in my seat. "I don't just want to make people see me. I want to make people see themselves. To believe in something more than they think they can." I take a deep breath. "I want to write. Like you do."

If I'd thought it was impossible to surprise my acting professor, apparently, I was wrong. Her eyes are wide and unblinking, as if I just spit a string of colorful curses onto her desk.

But she recovers, straightening.

"Your showcase piece," she says at last. "It was very moving. Writing, in the long run, is less about the words and more about the writer. A fresh voice, an interesting perspective. How honest they're willing to be with an audience."

I nod. "I understand. At least I think I do," I go on at her expectant look.

"Good. In that case, as penance for missing my class, I'd like you to write something for me."

---

My phone buzzes with a text as I head out of Talbot's office.

Tyler: It's done. I'm signed.

A wave of excitement rolls through me.

Annie: That's huge. We should celebrate. Tonight?

Tyler: I have a midterm tomorrow. We go out tonight, I'm getting zero studying done.

I can't resist teasing him.

Annie: I could have you in bed by midnight.

Tyler: I could have you against my dresser, in my shower, on my kitchen table.

Tyler: You could play me a song on my own guitar while you sit in my lap and I fuck you from underneath.

*Holy.* It takes every ounce of strength not to melt into a puddle in the middle of the hall.

Annie: Right. Ummm… tomorrow then?

Tyler: Deal. And I've got plans.

On impulse, I head to P69 and knock on the door. There's no answer. I'm turning away when the door cracks and Beck looks out at me in surprise.

"Hey, Manatee. You get the good word about my roomie's deal?"

"He just told me." I step inside and look over Beck's shoulder at his computer. "Damn. Half a million followers now. Are you going to keep posting about Tyler?"

He rubs a hand through his hair. "It's what they want."

There's a bit of sadness in his voice, and I fold my arms. "Well, I knew how good Tyler was, and I still followed your vlog for you."

His eyes crinkle at the corners. "Oh, I'm good with it. We sign up for the thousands of hours in places like this"—he gestures around the closet— "in the hopes that someday it'll come together. That someone'll see us and say, 'He's the one we've been looking for.'" His mouth curves. "I'm glad it's happening to Tyler."

I reach out a hand and run my fingers through his dark hair. "I see you, Beck. Don't give up."

"Back at you." He checks his watch. "It's still early in the day. My big break is waiting." His wink has me grinning. "Yours could be, too."

# Annie

"You look good," a familiar voice comments from the doorway as I step into my high heels.

I look up to see my roommate.

"Thanks, Rae." I glance between her and the fish on my desk. "I appreciate you looking out for Heath while I was gone. You didn't have to clean his bowl, too."

"I didn't."

I rise from the bed, smoothing down the silver dress that ends halfway down my thighs. I fold my arms across my chest. "Yeah, you did. But it's cool. You don't have to admit it."

She rolls her eyes, and I continue. "DJ Payne's playing in Brooklyn this weekend. I saw him on your playlist. Elle and I want to go, and we want you to come."

"I'll see what I can do." Her mouth purses. "Where are you going in the 'fuck me' dress?"

I grin. "Tyler's taking me out."

Rae arches a dark brow. "You guys have cool energy together. Don't take it for granted."

"Trust me, I won't ever take what we have for granted."

With one last look in the mirror, I head down for my date.

The last twenty-four hours after returning from LA have been a whirlwind.

After meeting Talbot yesterday, I got to work on her revised assignment. I was up all night and sent it by email at four in the morning. She wrote me back at five with a response that had my jaw dropping.

Now, it seems the surprises aren't over.

The limo outside the front doors can't be for me. But as Tyler emerges from the back seat, I know it is.

The driver gets out to hold the door, but Tyler waves him off.

"Are you kidding me?" I laugh, but before he can respond, I pull up short, taking in his pants, shined shoes, and tailored winter jacket. "Damn. This *is* a date. I'm impressed you found a peacoat. What's under it?"

Tyler unbuttons the coat with one hand and holds it open. The suit jacket underneath has me sucking in cold air that burns my lungs. "You dressed up. I'm kind of shocked."

His gaze roams up my bare legs, ending on my long jacket. "Your turn. Unless you're not wearing anything under that coat, in which case, fuck the date, we're going upstairs."

I unbutton the front of my coat, put both hands on my hips, and pose.

"Damn, Six." His voice is reverent, and I'm glad I sprung for the new dress. "You're stunning."

I feel myself flush in the dark. "Thanks."

His gaze drops to the necklace hanging between my breasts.

"Like your bling too."

"First boy I ever loved gave it to me. Never forgot it, or him."

Tyler's face fills with emotion as he helps me into the car. We talk on the ride, but he refuses to tell me where we're going. When the car pulls up and the driver holds my door open, I step out into lights as bright as day.

"Broadway!" I huff out a happy sigh.

Tyler shifts out after me, and as the car pulls away, he links his warm fingers through mine. "You asked me to a show a couple weeks ago, and I passed. I wanted to make it up to you."

The marquee on the theater has my eyes bugging out even more. "*Hamilton*? You're joking."

I start toward the doors, but our linked hands tug me back.

Tyler's eyes shine as he stares at me. "I love that about you," he murmurs.

"What?"

"You could have anything you want, and you're still thrilled by the world."

"The best things aren't about money," I remind him, smoothing a hand down the soft fabric of his coat. "Though if this is some male ploy to get me to sleep with you at the end of the night, it's not going to work."

The exposed bulbs cast Tyler's face in half shadow, and he has the decency to look offended.

"Don't sleep with me because I took you to *Hamilton*." He steps closer to let a stream of people past us, bending toward my ear and lowering his voice. "Sleep with me because you want to. Because even though the world's been offering you things this entire week, all you really want is to be alone with me."

I pull back to look him in the eye. "How about because I'm not wearing underwear?"

Tyler threads a hand into my hair, kissing me hard and hungrily.

"Fuck *Hamilton*," he grinds out, and I suck in an appalled breath.

"Absolutely not. We're going."

Tyler's groan vibrates through me. "Fine. But I'm feeling you up at intermission."

The theater is beautiful, and I love everything about it. It's opulent yet intimate, with plush red seats and arching gold decorations. Our seats are in the second row.

I point it all out to Tyler, and we discuss it until the lights go down.

From the opening number, I'm rooted in place.

So many stories are powerful, but this one grabs me and refuses to let go.

It's about building a legacy.

Taking action.

Fucking up.

Every word, every song, fills me as if I'm the one singing, and my lungs expand until I think my chest will burst.

It's beautifully, achingly human.

By the end, I feel reborn.

"Well?" Tyler asks when the ovation finishes and our row files out.

I don't move, staring at the stage after everyone's left our row. "This is it," I state. "This is what I want to do."

I cut a look up at Tyler's amused face. "Talbot sent me part of the book she's cowriting for a new musical. It's nearly finished, but she's been stuck on a couple of songs. I sent her some lyrics, just some spur-of-the-moment ideas, and she actually liked them. There's a chance I could work on it with her."

His grin is dazzling. Tyler wraps an arm around me, and we head down the aisle for the exit, my program tucked safely in my little bag like a perfect memory of tonight.

After the theater, the car takes us to a bar.

"Don't wait. We'll find our own way home," Tyler tells the driver when he lets us out, and we watch the car glide slowly down the street.

We reach the bar, and he holds the door. Inside, it's charming and funky, and we weave through the hip crowd and snag two stools.

We order from the bartender, and he returns a moment later with our drinks.

I lift mine as I consider. "To big dreams."

"To being so good they can't look away." Tyler's mouth tugs at the corner as if he's remembering the moment a year and a half ago when he gave me those words.

I take a sip of my drink, humming with pleasure at the smoothness as I glance around the bar.

"You hear anything from your dad?" Tyler asks.

Sadness edges into my excitement, though if I'm honest, a part of it's been there the past week, lingering in the corners of my mind, my soul. "Just Haley."

Tyler reaches over to rest a hand on my thigh. "He's not perfect, Annie, but none of us are. I know you've had your issues, and I don't agree with everything he does, but he loves the hell out of you."

Tyler's words have me sighing. "I know. And I probably should have told him. But I'm stubborn and so is he, and we both suck at backing down." I turn that over. "I told him about the letter from my birth mom. He was shocked. He almost looked... guilty. Like I caught him doing something he shouldn't."

"You could reach out to her."

"Maybe I will."

I scan the bar over his shoulder, the dozens of people drinking and laughing and joking. Is she somewhere doing the same thing right now?

I shake it off as my attention comes back to Tyler. Tonight's not for that—tonight is for us. "So," I start, my mouth twitching, "what does the future look like for Tyler Adams now that he has a record deal?"

His thumb strokes my thigh absently, sending little ripples of awareness through me. "Zeke wants me to record an EP to start. A combination of my own songs and a cover or two. I told him I wanted to record our songs, if you'd be open to that. The one from the showcase, and maybe we could work on more together."

Disbelief washes over me. "Tyler?! Yes. A million times, yes."

He grins at my response. "There's more, though." The brightness in his eyes dims a few watts. "The band I played with loved my sound, and they have a slot for an opener on their tour in a couple months. They want me to go with them. I have a couple days to decide."

My jaw drops. "Wow. That's huge."

"Two months ago, all I wanted was to get the hell out of Vanier. Now, I don't want to leave my friends or New York." He inspects the contents of his drink, then tosses it back in a single gulp before setting the glass down with a thud and meeting my gaze. "I don't want to leave you."

My chest warms at his admission.

"I feel as if I've always wanted you," he goes on, "and this is the first time I have you."

He reaches for my hand, and instead of threading his fingers through mine, he flips my palm. His thumb traces the lines of my palm in a way that feels far too intimate for public.

"Nothing can pull us apart if we don't let it," I promise softly, and his jaw tightens.

"Good."

He reaches into his pocket for something, holding it up. It glints between his fingers, the size of a nickel, but it's gold.

"What is that?" I ask.

"A promise." His voice goes rough as he stares at me. "I told you once I'd never leave you. I might have moved to New York last summer, but my heart never left you. I meant what I said. I mean it still."

My breath trembles out, unsteady.

"You are the only person I let under my skin," he goes on, his voice rough. "I've never felt about anyone the way I feel about you. The way you see the world, the way you care, the way you try, the way you get up when you're knocked down."

My throat is tight with emotion, and every word adds to the sensations overwhelming me.

"I choose you, Annie," he says. "Over uncertainty, over fear, over doubt. I will always choose you. Whether you're next to me or a thousand miles away, when you look at this, you'll know it's true."

I take the ring from him, and it's cool and heavy despite the narrow band. The inside is smooth, the outside scarred.

*No, carved.*

The band is engraved with flowers.

"It's beautiful," I manage.

Tyler rounds my stool and unfastens my necklace, then slips the ring over the chain and refastens the clasp. I adjust it, and the ring settles between my breasts along with the pressed flower. My fist closes around it.

I twist in my seat, needing to find his gaze. Once I do, it's so full of love and awe I never want to let it go.

I never want to let *him* go.

He claims my mouth in a long kiss that's searing and tender at once. By the time he pulls back, I'm tugging at his hair, needing to feel his body on mine.

"Let's get out of here," he murmurs. "That dress is killing me."

"I thought you liked it."

"I'm going to like taking it off you more."

We pay for our drinks before putting on our coats and stumbling outside.

"Let me call a cab."

"Come on," I tease, "we can walk."

With everything that's happened tonight, I could use the air.

I could inhale and entire city's worth of oxygen right now.

"So... sign, join, or jilt?" Tyler drawls as he holds the door, reminding me of our old game.

"Who?" I retort.

"Me."

I don't realize how late it is until we get into the street.

"Well," I say, pretending to consider. "You're already signed, so unless I lure you away from your label—"

"Which you could do in a heartbeat."

"Really?" I trip over the pavement, falling against his side with a laugh. "I have nothing to offer you."

His low chuckle buzzes through me. "Your mouth is remarkably persuasive."

"You'd leave Zeke for a blowjob?" I demand, mock aghast. The idea of Tyler coming apart under my hands, my mouth, is impossibly sexy.

He groans. "I'm walking home in the middle of the night with a fucking hard-on, and it's all your fault."

I laugh as we stumble down the road toward Tyler's place. He takes my hand as we talk about all kinds of things, our voices raised from the alcohol.

Nothing can break the beautiful imperfection of this moment. Despite the rift between me and my dad and the uncertainty of my future, Tyler's finally getting what he deserves, I'm learning to stand on my own feet, and we have each other.

We're a few blocks from his apartment, and I'm already imagining the things we're going to do together when a rough voice interrupts my fantasy.

"Give me your purse."

I glance at Tyler, sure I've misheard. "What did you say?"

But the words didn't come from him.

I spin to see a guy in black from head to toe. He's half in the shadows of the alley, which is why I didn't spot him. "Your purse. And phones."

Tyler moves between the guy and me, stilling when something under the guy's jacket glints in the streetlight.

My body goes cold. I don't know what it is, a knife or a gun, but every part of me's focused on that silver flash.

"Give it to him," Tyler says calmly, reaching into his pocket and holding out the phone.

*Give what? Shit. My bag.*

I swallow and force myself to hold out my purse with my phone inside. The man takes it and shoves it in his jacket. He hasn't touched me, but I feel violated, as if someone's burst our perfect bubble.

I cut a look down the street. The closest major intersection is five blocks away.

"Wallet too."

Tyler reaches slowly into his pocket and holds it out.

The guy takes it, flips it open to check for cash. "Got any jewelry?"

"No," Tyler answers steadily.

*How can he be so calm?*

"What about her?"

I shake my head fast. The man's gaze drops to my chest. My fingers close around the gold necklace.

"It's nothing," I say softly. "It was a gift."

"Hand it over."

My eyes burn as the ring and the rose warm in my hand. I can't move.

"Give it!" He makes a threatening gesture, and I hiccup a breath as I reach for the clasp with trembling fingers.

"No." Tyler's voice has an edge this time.

Something silver flashes again, and Tyler moves, every bit as fast at the other guy.

"The fuck you doing?!" the other guy shouts as Tyler lunges.

They're on the ground, and I'm watching in horror as they roll.

I want to scream, but it's stuck in my throat. It's like seeing a car crash. I can't call 9-1-1; he has my phone.

They roll over and over, and there's panting and grunting. Then the guy's out from under Tyler, sprinting down the sidewalk.

A sickening groan pulls me back.

"Tyler!" I drop to the ground next to him. One hand's still on my necklace, and I force myself to let go in order to roll Tyler onto his back.

The second I do, there's blood. The smell of it invades my nose, and I fight nausea as I search wildly for the source of it in the dark, patting his chest through his black dress shirt, rumpled and dusty from the fight.

"Tyler, oh my God. Say something."

His lips are parted, and the only thing that escapes is a grunt of pain.

Relief edges in as I shove Tyler's sweat-damp hair off his face, searching his half-lidded gaze.

I feel dampness around my knees, and my chin jerks down.

There's a bloom of red pooling at my leg near Tyler's side, and the moment I realize what's happened, the knot in my throat loosens.

Now, I scream.

---

Thank you for reading *A Love Song for Rebels*!

I hope you loved this second instalment of Tyler and Annie's epic, emotional story.

**If you can't wait for the exciting conclusion,
don't miss *A Love Song for Dreamers*.**

Dying to know how Tyler and Annie's relationship
went from friends to more?

Sign up for Piper Lawson's newsletter to get free
books, exclusive deals and more.

Plus you'll instantly receive *Love Notes*, the prequel
to *A Love Song for Liars*.

https://claims.prolificworks.com/free/p8Edk9gT

If you enjoyed *A Love Song for Rebels*, I'd be so grateful if you would leave me a 1-sentence review wherever you picked up this book. Then send me a link at piper@piperlawsonbooks.com so I can thank you personally!

---

**Rockstars don't chase college students...but Jax Jamieson's never followed the rules.**

Did you miss Jax and Haley's best-selling rockstar romance? You can binge the complete Wicked series today, beginning with *Good Girl*.

## THANK YOU

If you read *A Love Song for Rebels*…thank you. Thank you for trusting me with your time and emotions. Thank you falling in love with the beautiful, flawed, earnest characters that fill my mind from morning to night.

My readers are the most amazing readers in the world. You guys are positive, bold, enthusiastic, supportive, and amazing humans. I wouldn't write without you.

If you enjoyed *A Love Song for Rebels*, I'd be beyond grateful if you could take two minutes to leave a quick review wherever you picked it up. Reviews are like gold to us authors - especially indies!

If you do leave a review, I'd love to hear about it. Here're the best ways to reach out:
www.facebook.com/piperlawsonbooks
www.instagram.com/piperlawsonbooks
piper@piperlawsonbooks.com

Thanks for being awesome, for inspiring me every day, and for helping make it possible for me to do something I love.

xoxo

Piper

# BOOKS BY PIPER LAWSON



## OFF-LIMITS SERIES

*Turns out the beautiful man from the club is my new professor... But he wasn't when he kissed me.*

Off-Limits is a forbidden age gap college romance series. Find out what happens when the beautiful man from the club is Olivia's hot new professor.

## WICKED SERIES

*Rockstars don't chase college students. But Jax Jamieson never followed the rules.*

Wicked is a new adult rock star series full of nerdy girls, hot rock stars, pet skunks, and ensemble casts you'll want to be friends with forever.

## RIVALS SERIES

*At seventeen, I offered Tyler Adams my home, my life, my heart. He stole them all.*

Rivals is an angsty new adult series. Fans of forbidden romance, enemies to lovers, friends to lovers, and rock star romance will love these books.

## ENEMIES SERIES

*I sold my soul to a man I hate. Now, he owns me.*

Enemies is an enthralling, explosive romance about an American DJ and a British billionaire. If you like wealthy, royal alpha males, enemies to lovers, travel or sexy romance, this series is for you!

## TRAVESTY SERIES

*My best friend's brother grew up. Hot.*

Travesty is a steamy romance series following best friends who start a fashion label from NYC to LA. It contains best friends brother, second chances, enemies to lovers, opposites attract and friends to lovers stories. If you like sexy, sassy romances, you'll love this series.

## PLAY SERIES

*I know what I want. It's not Max Donovan. To hell with his money, his gaming empire, and his joystick.*

Play is an addictive series of standalone romances with slow burn tension, delicious banter, office romance and unforgettable characters. If you like smart, quirky, steamy enemies-to-lovers, contemporary romance, you'll love Play.

## MODERN ROMANCE SERIES

*When your rich, handsome best friend asks you to be his fake girlfriend? Say no.*

Modern Romance is a smart, sexy series of contemporary romances following a set of female friends running a relationship marketing company in NYC. If you enjoy hot guys who treat their families like gold, fun antics, dirty talk, real characters, steamy scenes, badass heroines and smart banter, you'll love the Modern Romance series.

# ABOUT THE AUTHOR

Piper Lawson is a WSJ and USA Today bestselling author of smart and steamy romance.

She writes women who follow their dreams, best friends who know your dirty secrets and love you anyway, and complex heroes you'll fall hard for.

Piper lives in Canada with her tall and brilliant husband. She's a sucker for dark eyes, dark coffee, and dark chocolate.

For a complete reading list, visit
www.piperlawsonbooks.com/books

**Subscribe to Piper's VIP email list**
**www.piperlawsonbooks.com/subscribe**

a amazon.com/author/piperlawson

BB bookbub.com/authors/piper-lawson

O instagram.com/piperlawsonbooks

f facebook.com/piperlawsonbooks

g goodreads.com/piperlawson

# ACKNOWLEDGEMENTS

I started to fall for Tyler and Annie in *A Love Song for Liars*, but in *A Love Song for Rebels*, they completely stole my heart. It moves me to see these two beautiful, flawed people grow and change and pursue their dreams the best way they know how.

That's what life is about.

So thank YOU for picking up this book and for trusting me to take you on a ride.

I promise it's one you'll remember for a long time.

This series wouldn't have happened without the support of my awesome advance readers. Extra shoutout to Beth, Tammy and Michelle for doing an early read!

Lori Jackson, Regina Wamba, and Kelley

Hawthorne Jefferson, thank you for the perfect cover.

Becca Mysoor, thank you for your on-point advice. Cassie Robertson and Devon Burke, thank you for questioning, polishing, and catching all the little things.

Thank you Dani Sanchez for getting the word out about my stories. And Annette Brignac and Michelle Clay... I would not be able to get these books to the people who matter most without your help.

Thank you all from the bottom of my heart. The best part of author life is having YOU in it.

xoxo

Piper

www.ingramcontent.com/pod-product-compliance
Lightning Source LLC
Chambersburg PA
CBHW051127190726
48290CB00006B/1730